The Lamentations of Julius Marantz

Unbridled Books

The Lamentations of Julius Marantz

Marc Estrin

The chapter "A Study of History" was first published in
Capitalism Nature Socialism, Volume 15, Number 1, March 2004, Joel Kovel, ed.

This is a work of fiction. The names, characters, places and incidents are either the product of the author's imagination or are used fictitiously, and any resemblance to actual persons living or dead, business establishments, events, or locales is entirely coincidental.

Unbridled Books
Denver, Colorado

Library of Congress Cataloging-in-Publication Data

Estrin, Marc.
The lamentations of Julius Marantz / Marc Estrin.
p. cm.
ISBN: 978-1-932961-38-6 (alk. paper)
1. Scientists—Fiction. 2. Reminiscing in old age—Fiction.
3. Science and civilization—Fiction. 4. Psychological fiction. I. Title.
PS3605.S77L36 2007
813'.6—dc22
2007021015

1 3 5 7 9 10 8 6 4 2

Book Design by SH.CV

First Printing

Contents

The Endgame Begins

Photos from a Family Album

À La Recherche d'une Femme Perdue

Endgame

The Lamentations of Julius Marantz

The Endgame Begins

1.

At the Movies

How lonely sits the city that was full of people. How like a widow has she become. She that was a princess among the cities has become a vassal.

—LAMENTATIONS 1:1

19 June 2003

The lights dimmed in Mini-Salle 7, the smallest and most hidden picture palace, deep in the warrens of Dodecaplex Two. Similarly had lights dimmed fifty years to the day before, dimmed that day at Ossining, New York, dimmed for Ethel Rosenberg as her husband was transmuted by an electric device not thirty yards away, and her own transformation beckoned.

House to half; house out. In the stepped dimming of the light, this day another Julius, a furtive Julius, a Julius on the lam, inspected the tiny chamber with its safely four, safely teenaged others. Though fifty years had passed, this other Julius, one Julius Marantz, was also scheduled for transfiguration—and for similar reasons.

WELCOME TO THIS EVENING'S
FEATURE PRESENTATION

Glitzy, shoddy graphics on screen, shocking to the dark-adapted eye.

SMOKING OF ANY KIND IS PROHIBITED
IN THIS THEATER

Three French maids in scanty, leggy dresses shake fingers No No No as a smoking cartoon biblical prophet pokes in from behind to baricroon, "Except, of course, for the Gold."

Maid One offers him a pack; Maid Two a light; Maid Three sidles herself up against his ashes and sackcloth. "High, but cool," she says as the others swoon in agreement.

"You can tell by the smell," Jeremiah says.

Julius Marantz settled in for an urgent interlude of safety. He had to catch his breath, gather his wits. Outside, sirens sang in trio and quartet, and Central Intelligence Corporation cars were everywhere, searching, no doubt, for him. His disguise was good. False white beard, filthy hippy clothes. Was it too late to consider cross-dressing? Jeremiah and his maids were floating up off screen. High, after all, was high.

BECAUSE THIS FILM IS ONLY SEVENTY MINUTES LONG, WE WILL HAVE OUR INTERMISSION RIGHT NOW. IF YOU HAVEN'T ALREADY, WE INVITE YOU TO CHECK OUT THE REFRESHMENT STAND IN THE LOBBY, WHERE YOU WILL FIND MANY DELICIOUS DRINKS AND SNACKS, INCLUDING THE U.S.'S OWN NATURAL FLAKES™. AND DON'T FORGET TO "GO FOR THE GOLD™®"!

House lights on. Damn! thought Julius, visible again. The four teenagers passed him, scuffing their largeness up the aisle. One picked and flicked a booger at the dirty old man while his buddies guffawed. "Santa Claus!" they taunted brilliantly.

Should I go out there? Julius wondered. Will it be suspicious to stay in here? Will the ushers be in to check refreshment receipts? Pascal's Wager. Not worth the consequences of a bad guess.

Julius limped up the aisle, practicing his crippled senior-citizen walk. At the stand he ordered up a Tub o' Pops™, in an arcane accent, and made his way back into the theater, careful not to spill the voluminous, olestrated popcorn suspended, crouton-like, in Diet-Pop™ Last to leave, first to return, he sat back down. The four teenagers marched in, laden with comestibles, just as the lights dimmed again. Though he had been only four years old at the time of Sing-Sing's dimming, he flashed, even now, on that event. Mommy and Daddy would not explain why they were crying.

House to half, house out. From the pentaphonic speakers: "Please rise and join in our national anthem." Drumroll. On the screen, Old Glory, version 52.6, flapping grandiloquently under a cross of David. The text on the staff, "YOUR LOGO HERE," Julius knew to be fraudulent. No way *his* logo—had he a logo—could make it onto Old Glory's white stripes. Those six spaces were available only to Fortune 500 companies, in the order of net income. And the image wasn't even up-to-date, for three days earlier, version 52.7 had appeared, with the top-two corporations switching places and the predicted supremacy of the Bank of Christ's logo.

A small animated hand—Michelangelo's Hand of God—pointed at the words as they scrolled along the bottom of the screen. So as not to attract attention, Julius stood and croaked along with his acned colleagues all the way to the final lines:

O'er the La-and of the Freeeeeee

(breathe)

To our Home . . . in the . . . Skies!

Above the flag appeared the dawning sun, which, in an amazing display of computer animation, morphed from red disk through each current flag logo, streaming from one to another in proper colors, into a glorious archangel who, opening his purple robe (like a cheap stripper, Julius thought), showed blazoned upon his chest in flaming letters

AND NOW, FOR OUR FEATURE
PRESENTATION . . .

Julius settled back for seventy minutes of he knew not what—but what did it matter? It was dark, he was unobserved and enveloped in the haze of Gold smoke from up front, he could pull down his mental ear flaps, shut his eyes. . . .

But wait! What was that up there, seen through the slit of his vision? The title of said Feature Presentation, typing out on screen in ancient Courier, with phony typewriter clacks, such as hadn't been heard since long before Microsoft became Macrosoft:

THE DAMNABLE LIFE AND DESERVÈD DEATH
OF JULIUS MARANTZ, SCIENTIST

A subway car, the IND, the very car he'd been in yesterday. He recognized the sequence of ads above the seat he'd finally obtained. "BEFORE THE END, COME BACK TO BUD," and "WHEN THE LORD

CALLS, WILL YOUR LINE BE BUSY?—FIBERCELLULARS™. USED IN THE OVAL OFFICE." A voice over the scene:

> THE MAN SHOWN HERE IS REAL AND KNOWN
> TO BE DANGEROUS. HE MAY EVEN NOW BE
> SEATED AMONG YOU. IF YOU SEE THIS MAN,
> CONTACT YOUR NEAREST CIC ATTENDANT
> OR CALL 1-888-TREASON. THANK YOU.

"The man" was shown in great detail: it was yesterday's Julius, clean-shaven, skin hennaed reddish-brown, seated in yesterday's jerking subway car, in old Levis and tie-dyed Grateful Dead T-shirt, carrying the "Smart People for Central Intelligence" plastic bag he used for his costume changes, the one with the smiley face wearing glasses, just like the one now at his feet.

Feigning uncontrollable hiccups through the lobby, he was out of that theater in a flash, out onto the mean streets, the scorching sidewalks of New York. Would that this light would dim as well.

2.

GEKO

27 January 2001

Julius," the Vice-President had said, "we want you to give us the rights to your machine."

"Who's we?"

"GEKO," said the priest.

"Geheimniskoalition," the Vice-President translated.

Julius surveyed the wrinkled faces dotting the Office of Counter-terrorism Operations, xanthotic raisins in a high-tech scone.

"I'm sorry. Shall we go round the circle and do introductions?" The Vice-President was always polite.

"Daryl Plunk, Korea desk, Birthright Foundation."

"General Plunk is part-time DOD, retired."

"Carolyn Worthington, Earth Friends." She looked the very model of the upright Quaker she was.

"You're next," the VP urged.

"Oh. Julius Marantz."

"Organization?"

“Middlebury College, um Physics Department.”

“Edgar?”

“Edgar X. Thornbottom, Society of Jesus, World Council of Churches. Call me Thorn.”

“Thorn.” Julius nodded.

“As in crown of.”

GEKO laughed.

Julius said, “Um.”

“Morton Plumpe, Thompson Kline and Plumpe.”

“Our K Street representation.” GEKO nodded collectively at the vice-presidential savoir faire. “And this is Cosma McMoon, our court stenographer.”

“Hi.”

Julius was wary. “Is this a court?”

“A court of appeal, you might say,” the Vice-President clarified. “We’re appealing to you to consider what’s best for your country.”

“And for the world,” Ms. Worthington added.

“And for you,” said Thorn. This last was offered as spiritual direction, not threat.

“We want you to give us the rights to . . . you know,” the Vice-President repeated.

“The Doodad.”

“Yes.”

“Why don’t you just take it? You have . . .”

“Julius, this is America. We don’t just . . .”

"The overriding question is one of intellectual property rights," Advocate Plumpe advised. "Don't you agree?"

Julius had been led through the serpentine corridors of the Executive Office Building, down, down, down, and around to the once-domain of Ollie and Fawn, following conduits from State, Defense, and Intelligence to the Situation Room beyond all situations, the external Executive brain.

As they walked past a mock-horror-film poster touting *The Return of Al Gore,* not visible, of course, to blindfolded Julius, the Vice-President, his elbow in hand, had reflected on the general condition:

"It's not just you, Julius. We are all of us blinded—by this world. We have lost our expectancy, our sense of clairvoyance, and night advances swiftly upon us." It was sound bites such as this that gave the country confidence in the man a heartbeat away. Beepers beeped buzzers, and locks fell away. Julius was seated in a chair and his blindfold removed. His eyes adjusted quickly to the opulent dimness of a room packed with panels, winking at him like a Hydra-headed trollop.

"Julius, all of us here realize that we're living in tough times. Don't you agree?" The Vice-President placed a confidential hand on his shoulder. "Don't you?"

Julius gave a noncommittal grunt.

"And people are yearning for something different, an era of peace, love, and unity. But their world is empty, Julius. It's a world of memorials without memory. Ours is a time of brainless arrogance in which our cosmic tragedy is repackaged as entertainment."

"What has the Doodad got to do with all this?" its inventor asked.

"Nothing. And everything," the Vice-President said.

Thorn stepped up to bat.

"Julius, you are a religious man. You know we must strive to remake, by our own God-given powers, the world that our Father has made for us out of nothing and given us as our workshop."

"You see the Doodad as remaking the world?"

"More like transforming it, Julius. Just look around. It's survival of the sleaziest, wouldn't you say? Hedonism 'Я' Us. Good God, six of the seven deadly sins are now virtues! Greed, avarice, and envy have become the keys to advancement. Gluttony, luxury, and pride are emblems of success. OK, sloth we don't value—yet—but we're on the way. Never has there been so little feeling of the Sacred as a genuine power.

"God blesses and serves America. But where is the demand that Americans first of all serve God, or make any real sacrifice? Look at the garbage piling up in the streets. It's God's metaphor. He's trying to get our attention."

There was a pregnant pause. The others nodded, as if the conclusion were obvious.

"And?"

"And you can help Him."

"I can help God?"

"He needs your help."

"I'm just a physicist, Mr. Thorn."

"*To call heaven's rich unfathomable mines (Mines, which support archangels in their state) Our own! To rise in science, as in bliss, Initiate in the secrets of the skies!* Edward Young," said Edgar X. Thornbottom.

"What he means," the Vice-President explained, "is that we no longer live in the times of Galileo and Giordano Bruno. Religions no longer suppress revolt; they have long since become integrated into technological society."

"What do you mean 'revolt'?"

"*Re-voltare.* As in *teshuvah,* Hebrew for turning." Thorn's explication of text.

"Oh. I thought you meant *I* was revolting—um, rebelling."

"No, no. Why would I say that?" Thornbottom continued. "I just meant in our materialist age of Kali Yuga, now drawing to a close, people want—need—the magic and security of something that's beyond them, something greater, something more, something guided, perhaps, by advanced beings, angels maybe, or emissaries from an extraterrestrial civilization. There needs to be a mass ascension to new realms of consciousness."

"And that's where you come in—or rather, your Doodad does," the Vice-President clarified.

"Is this some sort of search for ET?"

"No, Julius, for mass ascension."

A whiff of burning sulfur. Yet from those flames no light, but rather darkness visible.

"You want to use the Doodad for mass ascension?"

"Look," said Carolyn Worthington, "the population is exploding, and there is a huge ozone hole. Do you see how those fit together?"

"No."

"Find a hole and fill it?"

"You mean you want to fill the ozone hole with excess population?"

A group silence of affirmation.

"Some of us do," said Ms. Worthington.

"You want me to use the Doodad to shoot people up to fill the ozone hole? Live people?"

"Protein molecules absorb the ultraviolet," General Plunk informed him.

"Wouldn't the people get a little . . . sunburned?"

"By the time they need SPF 40, they'll have expired."

"And after they are burned to a crisp?"

"The molecular cloud will do nicely," the General informed him. "Or so I'm told."

The whiff had grown from smell to stench. Four humans stared at Julius. Another stared at her stenographic screen. Julius's breathing was shallow and fast.

"I see," he said.

"You'll surely agree there's a population problem." Plumpe asserted.

Julius nodded.

"Population pollution problem," Carolyn added.

His nodding continued.

"Well, then?" the Vice-President asked.

There was a long pause in the room. Julius looked around.

"Who is to choose the victims?"

"Mortals," said Thornbottom. "We are *all* mortal. Some must watch, while some must sleep. . . ."

"GEKO will make the selections," General Plunk explained. "Naturally, those selections will be weighted against America's enemies. I assume you'd have no objection to that?"

Julius was silent.

"Enemies both foreign and domestic."

"I see."

"Julius," Thornbottom advised, "this cannot be an easy life. We all have a tough time keeping our minds open and deep, keeping our sense of beauty, our ability to see it in places remote and strange; we have a tough time keeping open the many intricate paths in a great open, windy world; but this, as I see it, is the human condition; and in this condition we can help, because we can love one another. We must free our souls from the everyday, and open them to the *influxus mentium superiorum.*"

"Let me see if I understand this," Julius said. "You want to use the Doodad to lift your enemies up into the sky."

"*Our* enemies, Julius."

"Um, *our* enemies."

"And to turn people to God," the Vice-President added, "which would make for a better world. Don't you agree?"

"Why will this turn people to God?"

His interlocutor was truly astonished. "Julius, you don't need to be a rocket scientist to understand that *this* is the Rapture. Long-awaited, long-expected great reward. Who will get the credit? God."

"But that would be a lie—a hoax!"

Plumpe shook his head. "None of the higher religions include *lying* among the mortal sins. There is no simple commandment: Thou shalt not lie."

The Vice-President stood up from his chair and began pacing the room, his hands clasped, Beethoven-like, behind him.

"Whatever may be meant by moral landscape, Julius, at the moment, the best of our natures is drowning in the worst. Have you noticed how many people are simply nuts? This simple action will inject moral ballast to right the listing ship."

"To stabilize the world."

"To ease the population."

"To harmonize with friends."

"This is not a question of old teachings in new forms but of total reformulation in light of present experience."

"Bird of prey to bird of prayer."

"Per aspera ad astra."

"Julius, millions of children are starving to death each month," Carolyn Worthington said. "There are now one hundred seventeen wars being fought across the planet, and massive breakdowns of social and political structures. Can it get worse? Can it not only get better? The Rapture—real or fabricated—corresponds to our most fundamental cravings. We'll be making a new Truth."

Morton Plumpe gently placed paper on clipboard and handed it to Julius, along with an antique Parker '51, Plumpe's personal treasure.

"Julius, this is a letter of permission. It will enable us to use the Doodad to bring order to the world. Your world. Your children's world."

Julius sat there, paralyzed. He had no children. Four pairs of eyes bore down upon him. The Vice-President offered his penultimate gambit, well-rehearsed.

"My friend, after the Declaration of Independence was signed, John Page wrote to Thomas Jefferson, 'We know the race is not to the swift nor the battle to the strong. Do you not think an angel rides in the whirlwind and directs this storm?'"

Julius didn't know whether he was supposed to answer the question.

"Much has changed since that fateful time, Julius. But Jefferson would still recognize the monumental themes of the day, America's grand story of courage, and its simple dream of dignity. We are not this story's author, yet His purpose is achieved in our duty, and our duty is fulfilled in His service. Never tiring, never yielding, we can renew that purpose today, to make our country more just and generous, to affirm the dignity of our lives. The work continues. The story goes on. And an angel still rides in the whirlwind and directs this storm. God bless you, Julius Marantz, and God bless America."

Plumpe proffered the Parker once again, and Julius took it. The room held its breath. When no signature was forthcoming, the Vice-President was forced to use the last of his resources.

"Julius, you are a scholar. Consider, then, the Lord Chancellor of the Realm, Sir Thomas More, who steadfastly rejected each petition of the King of England; who therefore was beheaded and his head lodged upon a pole on London Bridge. Would you care to reflect on this?"

The Uncertainty Principle itself was not as uncertain. But he took the Parker and engraved the paper with his own name: Julius Marantz.

Salvator mundi? Diabolus providebitor? Or simple *Homo ignavus et stupidus?*

The Thomas More bit was stricken from the record.

Lamentation on the Loss of Self and the Fall of Man

When my dog, Yenta, was hit by a car shortly after her bark mitzvah, my family went into heartfelt mourning and even had me say the Kaddish for her. *Yitgadal v'yitkadash,* and all that. Several months later, as a lower-maintenance replacement, we got a young gray cat my father named Bubastis and my mother and I called Bubeleh.

Bubastis did not wag her tail or jump up and down in joy. When you called her, she pretended not to hear. When you offered food, she would take a minute or so before deigning to investigate. Truly a goddess, as in the ancient days of Amenhotep, meditating on the sublime.

A serene and haughty deity, yes—until perchance my mother might rip apart an old knitted sweater to reclaim the wool for future knitting. Then Bubastis transformed instantly into Bubeleh, fell from her Olympian heights—or whatever heights the Egyptian gods had once inhabited—fell to clownish, buffoonish depths.

She would bat incessantly at the outspooling strands, and when they were captured, she would roll on her back and bite and kick at them as if they might be emblems of Set, brother of Osiris and god of chaos and evil. The same behavior could be brought on by a dropped button.

What a fall was there! What a self-forgetting! The Bubastis-Bubeleh conversion was my first real spur to seriously contemplate "the Fall of Man."

Consider the humans who inhabited that room deep in the bowels of the EOB. Executives aspiring to become executioners. Was there not a similar fall involved—with far greater consequences? A most costly disorder of self-forgetting?

Though among themselves they dubbed it only "the Big Fib," these men and women endorsed the largest kind of lies—lies based on ultimate half-truths centuries out of repair. Why must the best and brightest devote themselves so zealously to world suicide? Because they had spent their mature lives in constant contemplation of the silicon chip? Is our global tragedy merely the sum of their individual failings, men and women busily fondling their self-esteem? The road to hell is paved with bad intentions.

So here we are all in the crisis-strewn City Paranoiac, enacting the primal passion play, engaged in wars to end all peace—the American way of evading life.

And what of me? Was I so innocent? Was not embracing science a profound and protracted crisis of the imagination?

As Bubastis was transformed into Bubeleh by a mere wisp of wool, so I, trying to drag at least one foot out of the insurmountable severity of an inhuman world, transformed myself from *Homo sapiens* to *Homo monstrosis,* selling the doodad that is my soul to GEKO's empty truths, slogans, philosophies, morality, religion, and codes—all of them in a key foreign to what once was my own or my father's. My guilt goes deeper than politics.

Being in perpetual flight from reality requires far too much. I am exhausted, tacking against the mighty wind that is the wrath of God.

The winner must lose, but must the loser win? *Jerusalem, Jerusalem, convertere ad Dominum.*

3.

Contragravitas

She weeps bitterly in the night, tears on her cheeks, among all her lovers she has none to comfort her; all her friends have dealt treacherously with her, they have become her enemies.

—LAMENTATIONS 1:2

At Fourteenth Street, in the cool safety of the IRT, Julius's car filled to excess with a dozen blissed-out choral beggars, one of the many groups of ragged singers, now of a sudden flourishing in the all-consuming religious frenzy around them. The sopranos all looked lean, with long, stringy hair, while the altos seemed plumper, better-fed, with short dark curls. The tenors and basses were indistinguishable, all with scraggly beards and too-small short-sleeved shirts, their eyes shifty, even in ecstasy.

Ten thousand times ten thousand, they sang,
In sparkling raiment bright,

The armies of the ransomed saints

Throng up the steeps of light.

And very loudly they sang, bawling nasally at the tops of their lungs, forte to fortissimo, pitch and amplitude well-suited to the fierce background noise of the New York subways. After one verse, having established their religioartistic bona fides, out came the begging cups: McDonald's, Dunkin' Donuts, arches now angel wings and donut hole now fitting snugly on a saint in sugary halo. They fanned out into the crowd, picking their way through, occasionally stumbling over bodies of the sleeping homeless and near-dead who lolled and sprawled on the filthy linoleum floor. Even the least of these lepers, like most of the other passengers, were plugged into various types of headsets and heard the choral tune as background counterpoint to the rumble, rock, and rap already driving their befuddled neuro-transmitters.

'Tis finished! all is finished,

Their fight with death and sin:

Fling open wide the golden gates,

And let the victors in.

Standing at Julius's knees, a small boy, frightened by the singers, cried, "Up, Mommy, up, up, up" at his strap-hanging, ignoring mother, and clutched a stuffed plush crucifix to his chest. Julius smiled sympathetically at him, but the false beard, shabby clothes, and henna-blotched skin did little to pacify the child. Mom, minimally protective, pushed him around toward her rear, six inches farther from the bad man.

To relieve her strain and suspicion, Julius cast his glance away through the forest of bodies bunched and clumped in the swaying car, most dressed in stretchy, clingy clothing embroidered with corporate logos and slogans: GET YER TLC FROM THE CIC; HÄAGEN-ZIEGFRED CHOCOFIXION CRUNCH®, a flock of sportswear swishes™ swooshing skyward; a HEAVENFIRST!®er kicking an offending Earthist in the behind.

What rush of hallelujahs
Fills all the earth and sky!
What ringing of a thousand harps
Bespeaks the triumph nigh!

An ethereal soprano wearing a paper crown shoved her Burger King o' Kings® cup under Julius's nose, reaching around the mother and child. Her face, like many others, was painted in opaque pinkish sunblock, hers, though, with blue winged hearts on each cheek. Julius deposited a Susan B. Anthony dollar in her cup, and so grateful was she for his largesse that she pushed her head between him and Mom's abdomen, and making tender eye-contact-in-depth, she sang, for him alone, the next verse:

O day, for which creation
And all its tribes were made!
O joy, for all its former woes
A thousandfold repaid!

Julius smiled wanly back and pulled his eyes from hers to study the advertising high across the aisle. WE WILL BE CAUGHT UP IN THE CLOUDS TO MEET THE LORD IN THE AIR. (THESSALONIANS 4:17) U.S. CHURCH OF GOD. As Alison (for that was the soprano's name) had not taken the hint and was still singing sweetly of joy into the back of her benefactor's head, Julius turned to look at her again and said, "We will be caught up in the clouds to meet the Lord in the air."

"Yes, oh, yes," she interpolated between pitches, gave him a peck on the cheek, and moved on. As he watched her go, an image on one of the infomercial screens caught his eye. . . . THE FORTHCOMING BLESSINGS OF POWER AND FREEDOM© . . . and then it was gone, replaced by a star-studded minitalk on the virtues of U.S. Natural Flakes™.

Julius looked around him, feeling searingly responsible for the mindless squalor of the car and its inhabitants. IT IS TO REMIND STUDENTS OF THE BLESSINGS FORTHCOMING, the stone had said, WHEN A SEMI-INSULATOR IS DISCOVERED IN ORDER TO HARNESS GRAVITY AS A FREE POWER AND REDUCE AIRPLANE ACCIDENTS. There it stood, still, in his mind, as odd as it had been the day he had first toured the campus. THIS MONUMENT HAS BEEN ERECTED BY THE GRAVITY RESEARCH FOUNDATION, ROGER W. BABSON, FOUNDER. 1960.

A monument to the future and not to the past, to a future impossible to imagine. The stone was dismissed by the physics faculty as a small price to be paid for six figures' worth of stock buried beneath it, which, when exhumed thirty-five years later, ten times increased in value, had provided a massive down payment on the new physics building where Julius had so recently worked. Academic cynicism, you may say. Coddle the codger and get his bucks. Yet there were a few visionaries at Middlebury, and in the larger physics community, who intuited a method beyond the oddball madness of Roger W. Babson.

Julius's teacher Dick Feynman had been one of them. "Look," he had told his class of Cal Tech grad students back in '64, "I don't know nothin' about geometry. I stink at geometry. But I'm good wit' particles, and so are you. And so . . ."—here he did a small-scale drumming act on the old wooden desk—"let's get rid of this general relativity stuff, and do some *particles*."

It was a great moment in the history of science. The study of gravity had been stuck in the cave where Einstein had left it, unsolved, and the entrance hole had grown smaller and smaller as physicists gravitated to work with the huge new accelerators. True to his word, Dick and his kids had developed a whole new theory, with equations and Feynman diagrams to go with it—gravity not as the curved geometry of space-time but as the energy of particle exchange, gravitons passing in and out of systems. "Guess what, gang," he'd said. "The equations come out the same as the old man's."

Why was this even on Feynman's agenda? Roger W. Babson. Maybe. The man behind the stone. He was a nutcase, to be sure. He had run for President of the United States against FDR on the New Prohibition Party ticket. He wanted voters tested on their understanding of issues before they could cast a ballot. He vetted his students' choices of mates. and was convinced a businessman could learn all he needed to know about the arts and literature in a couple of months. He spent his money in strange ways, buying and shipping, board by board, Isaac Newton's study to Babson College in Wellesley, Massachusetts, and Newton's apple trees, too. Yes, he had lost loved ones, two of them—to gravity, he thought. Not plane crashes, as the stone might suggest, but drowning. So, with characteristic determination, he set out to defeat it. Over the course of ten years, his $1,000 annual prize for the best essay on gravity or antigravity (this at a time when full professors of physics were making only $5,000) began to attract serious thinkers, diverting the subject from the exclusive province of weirdo inventors of hovercrafts and perpetual-motion machines. When Julius began with Feynman in '72, the theoretical work was already advanced: the theory remained to be tested.

Who could mess with the geometry of the universe? Who but the earth and the sun, and other quite massive individuals? Not a mere 160-pound weakling like Julius. On the other hand, particles, Julius thought, meant rays, and rays, if powerful enough . . .

But that was years ago. What Julius's power and freedom had come to was now sitting in a fake beard on the IRT in a brand-new century, watching a child hiding behind his mother, sucking on a red stuffed plush crucifix. Julius, our limping hero. Julius on the lam. Across the way sat a purple-haired rider wearing a prisoner costume with angel wings. His expression was blissful. Julius's was not.

ALEPH

The Limping Hero

It's hard to be on the lam with a limp, a limp not just of his truncated right foot but, worse, of his addled right brain, the half responsible for conceiving wholes.

"On the lam" is an interesting expression. Some think it came from the Baron Herman K. Lamm, a German émigré bank robber killed by the police in 1930, who had developed an elaborate theory of getaways, ultimately passed on by his boys to John Dillinger. And yes, Julius had robbed a bank: the Bank of Anteus, the bank of connection to the earth. Why should he not be pursued?

But the limp. Far more interesting is the limp. Julius was born imperfect. So are we all. And, imperfect, he no longer qualified for Paradise (neither do we). Some pleasures, yes; we may snag a few—along with our pain, degradation, and finally death.

Julius, like us, earned his living by the sweat of his brow and, it turns out—collateral damage—the death of multitudes. Of this last, many of us are spared.

Limpers. Jacob had a limp from wrestling with an angel. The Devil may also have a limp. It's the cloven feet. Richard III, Schlepfuss, developed a particularly worrisome response:

I, that am curtailed of this fair proportion,
Cheated of feature by dissembling Nature,
Deformed, unfinished, sent before my time
Into this breathing world, scarce half made up,
And that so lamely and unfashionable
The dogs bark at me as I halt by them;
Why, I, in this weak piping time of peace,
Have no delight to pass away the time,
Unless to spy on my shadow in the sun
And descant on mine own deformity:
And therefore, since I cannot prove a lover,
To entertain these fair well-spoken days,
I am determined to prove a villain.

Julius, also a Schlepfuss, was determined not to prove anything of the kind. Yet he did.

For each of us, there are ten thousand doors leading out into limitless fields of betrayal. We take them as they come, not knowing what it will mean to open them, to leap out into an unknown life. Some of us shy instantly away from the sight we see, the path from out the doorway. Most of us are content to live—if not quite in quiet desperation, then among vague shadows of affable, mild discomfort, avoiding both the fierce light of bliss and the pitch black of despair, shades seeking temperate shade. We shield ourselves from the extreme.

But this incorruptible has put on corruption. And his shield is coming to bits. The lame Hephaestus will no longer protect him. Nor will his high place in science, even his Nobel nomination, protect him. He did not offer his achievement up to Mammon; he did not wrap himself in it for caress or protection; he does not identify with "greatness." So greatness will not protect him.

Julius Marantz was once a researcher, a creator, not a monster. If Saturn introduced agriculture to Rome and founded its Capitol, he also castrated his father and ate his children. Julius didn't.

Nevertheless.

Who was this man? How does he come to be riding the Lexington Avenue express this day in June, disguised in filthy clothes and a false beard? Has his life, in fact, always been one of limping, of hiding, a life on the lam?

Photos from A Family Album

4.
Young Julius Marantz

"Sir Isaac told me that when he was born he was so little they could put him into a quart pot & so weakly that he was forced to have a bolster all around his neck to keep it on his shoulders."

—JOHN CONDUITT, KEYNES-NEWTON MS. 130

KING'S COLLEGE, CAMBRIDGE.

The birth of a child is often a shock. Comes a normal head—shock enough in its massiveness and massively violated sensibilities. The tiny shoulders are less prepossessing, but there follows the somehow shocking fiveness of fingers, and the ten tiny nails. Then the meteorite impact of its sex, modest in the female, but alarmingly large and blue in a male. Where might that monster insert itself? But in the case of Baby Boy Marantz, the greatest astonishment came to an already overwhelmed parent almost as an aftershock—the distal third of the infant's right foot was missing. Not five toes, not four, but no toes. A forefoot ending in a tiny Popsicle stump, cute enough to suck on, but alarming nevertheless.

Since the newborn was curled so tightly in fetality, the truncation was not initially noticed. But when his first slap evoked his first (and only) barbaric yawp, a chief fact of his life became obvious enough: of the two chicken legs by which he was suspended, only one had claws.

The doctor was kind, in a physician-like sort of way, if a little New Agey for Christmas morn. "Your baby is very special," he told Florence, who was still so focused on her son's son-ness as not to have noticed his feet. But by the time she rendezvoused with her husband, Phillip, in the recovery room, she was tearful and distraught over "amniotic banding," a term she hadn't imagined she'd ever hear. When asked whether they wanted the child circumcised, only Phillip was in a state to answer: "Yes, of course." It was, after all, Brooklyn Jewish Hospital.

Why was the baby so tightly curled? A typical Julius overreaction, even at so tender a negative age. Initially quite active, even combative, and longing, as ever, for freedom, fetal Julius kicked his way through Florence's amniotic sac.

But his was a freedom fraught with dangers. It was sheer good luck that doled out only a *partial* congenital amputation of the guilty foot. Chorionic fibers floating in the uterine fluid enveloped that fast-growing tissue, strangled it, and choked its blood supply. Because the tear was high in the sac, the rest of Julius's body was spared the contest of bare nekked versus fibrous placenta, a cruelly lopsided encounter.

Florence blamed herself for playing tennis till halfway through the pregnancy. Her penance was to become a guilt-ridden, overbearing, domineering, oppressive Jewish mother to her now withdrawn son, a strategy not likely to ameliorate his problems. Had he cut his mother's heart out in a fit of rage, her bleeding corpse would have warned him to be careful with that sharp knife.

But Julius would never have cut out her heart. Julius would never even get angry. Julius's overreaction to his own early kick was rarely to kick out again—with some notable exceptions. Had he been born later, he would quite likely have been labeled autistic and treated with megavitamins or special schools. As it was, he demonstrated the mild characteristic symptoms of withdrawal from others, which earned him the title of "genius" from resentful schoolmates and admiring aunts.

Julius was named not for maternal Grandpa Julius but for Julius Caesar. An odd gift, you might say, but it was a gift from an odd father. Somehow he thought that by naming his firstborn son Julius, someone or something might be appeased. It was the missing foot. A crippled child, he thought, had better bear an appellation of power, or he would be trampled by the bipedal world. Had not Sid Caesar been catapulted from saxophone to stardom? By private analogy,

Julius Marantz might do the same. But why not name him "Ike," then, or "Franklin," or "Martin Buber," after the star of his Jewish philosophy class—figures of majesty unalloyed? Because Phillip also wanted his son to grow up with a warning in his very name about the destructive potential of unlimited power.

Phillip's son had been a physicist since the moment his allowance had afforded a regular purchase of *Popular Mechanics.* While the other boys were sneaking peeks at hidden *Playboys,* Julius was ogling certain curvaceous diagrams in *Scientific American.* He built airplanes of great complexity, flying models of balsa and tissue, powered at first by rubber bands and flying free, and later by tiny gasoline engines, flying circles around their puppet master, who pulled their strings and controlled their pitch. "How can metal airplanes fly?" he wanted to know, and Phillip's "They have engines" did not suffice. Off to the library. Ten-year-old Julius's subsequent dinnertime lecture/demonstration on Bernoulli's Principle was impressive. But Julius would not repeat it for Show and Tell and continued to get "Needs Improvement" on the "Plays Well with Others" section of his report card.

There was something else. Visions. Supernatural visions, usually involving flying. For his eighth birthday, Phillip and Florence took Julius to his first Broadway show, Mary Martin and Cyril Richard in *Peter Pan.* "Wires," he said. He knew right away it was wires. Florence: "No, Julius—it's magic. The fairy dust makes them fly." It was at that moment that Julius Marantz condensed his attitude toward his mother and perfected his withering sneer.

Nonetheless, the play had repercussions in dreamland. Into Julius's bedroom that night came flying a huge figure—not Peter Pan but Captain Hook. It was definitely Hook. You could tell by the hook. It was holiday time, and Hook arrived with a bag of Hanukah gelt for Julius if he would join the uprising. He said he had lost his foot, the right foot—same as Julius's—to a great whale that had spit him up, here at Julius's house, on the shores of Ninevah. If Julius would come with him, he would heal the boy's foot, or carve him a great peg leg out of ivory. Or he would teach Julius to fly.

Julius said yes, he would go, and soon awoke in fright, not from Hook but from stomach-swoops during his first out-of-body experience, an adventure-world he learned to tame and master. OOB. Ooooooooooob!

5.

Science for Beginners

In the beginning, there was potential energy. Or at least that was what Philip Marantz said to his five-year-old as they creaked and clanked up the Cyclone's lift hill to eighty-five feet above the boardwalk. To their right, the beach and the sea; to their left, the Stilwell Avenue subway station, elevated, and Nathan's Original Hot Dogs, 35¢.

First car—nothing but the best for Philip's terrified boychik, who had waited two whole years to be five and old enough. The last words Julius heard before he went into free fall were "kinetic energy"—and then the drop, eighty-five feet at sixty degrees, whizzing toward unshielded catastrophe at sixty miles per hour. During six tight turns, eighteen crossovers, and eleven more drops, Philip yelled to him about "centrifugal" and "centripetal," but aside from fleeting notions of fugues and flowers, all Julius could think about—with the fiercest certainty—were three truths less abstract: first, his immediately approaching death; next, his dissolution as a skin-bound entity; and finally, at the last few elevations, the incomprehensible Satanic guilt, the Abrahamic cruelty of his father, who had taken him up on the mountain to apply the knife of forces to his gorge. When the three cars rolled into their shed, Julius looked at his father and said, "Let's do it again."

Satanic. Abrahamic. Large concepts for a small, thin child. His first bedtime book had been *Goodnight Moon,* that enormous poesis of mittens and kittens, of brush, mush, and hush, his mother had read to him over and over. But his second book—first of the fatherly reign—was not *Pat the Bunny* or even *Chicken Little;* it was *Paradise Lost.* Julius was the only four-year-old in Coney Island who could declaim at the birthday parties of his peers,

> Him the Almighty Power
> Hurl'd headlong flaming from th' ethereal sky
> With hideous ruin and combustion down
> To bottomless perdition, there to dwell
> In adamantine chains and penal fire,
> Who durst defy th' Omnipotent to arms.

He liked that one. Other parents were jealous and impressed. His third book was *Bible Stories for Young Adults* (with parental commentary), his fourth *Fear and Trembling* (selections). Philip had plans for his bedtime boychik.

By the fourth Cyclone ride, physiology had been suspended, or at least relegated to proper minority, and Julius and Philip were able to experiment with outbreath versus inbreath, screaming versus silence, standing (briefly) versus sitting, eyes shut versus open, looking backward versus forward. They had even discussed, en route, the shouted possibility of Julius's getting married on a roller coaster, though the whole idea of marriage was still, to him, outré and disgusting. "No" was his answer.

On land, Phillip was loaded for pedagogical bear. Still staggering off the Cyclone, he pulled from his pocket three marbles and a little ball of string. Using his earflapped hat as a container, he created an impromptu centrifuge, the first of many swinging things on strings, sometimes including in their construction small spring-scales which Julius found impossible to read. But he got the idea: the balance of centrifugal and centripetal forces. Newton's third law.

He of the three laws played a large part in childe Julius's life as a large-headed, weak-bodied, doppelganging sibling, later incarnated as Julius's pet lizard, which he bought on the boardwalk from a red-headed clown with a set of strong white teeth hawking, "Charming gentleman for sale," which turned out to be a grotesquely appealing eyelashed, or Satanic, gecko, *Uroplatus phantasticus.* The name "Newton" seemed obvious to Julius, since the quadruped could walk on ceilings, though his namesake, for all his power, had never been known to do so.

"How much?"

"How much you got?"

Fishing in pockets.

"A quarter."

"Sold."

But it was not the Cyclone that most called forth the great Sir Isaac; it was, of course, the Parachute Jump, what Philip called the I-Fall Tower, that cross between art deco and military-industrial, recently migrated to Brooklyn from Queens. With lap bar down and his father's arm to keep him from slipping through, Julius would begin the 250-foot ascent, more than three times the Cyclone's height, his club foot swinging like a tiny pendulum in a huge grandfather clock. Father and son would rotate their rides around the compass points, noting the landward landmarks and the seaward lack of them, ominous, mysterious. The sounds faded away until all they could hear was the wind-harp song of the cables. It was coming, he knew—the fall, whoosh, to Steeplechase Park, Julius, the falling apple of his father's eye.

From morn
to noon he fell, from noon to dewy eve,
A summer's day; and with the setting sun
Dropp'd from the zenith like a falling star—

Though they hit the shocks in about the time it took to say the verse, there was time during the lift to talk of many things—of potential and kinetic energy to be sure, but also of rising and falling, and upness and down, of the cloud about their ears and the cloud of unknowing, and about the possibility of a wedding in free fall. The answer again was "No." How could anyone be owned by another person when he was owned by gravity? "What made you want to be a physicist?" Julius was often asked. The answer was obvious.

An interesting gang of kids colonizing the streets, the park, the boardwalk, over and under it, and the beach: Smokey Bleeker, Danny the Bull, Ershky, Spooky Weiner, Marvin, Davey, Louie, Danny the Count, Mickey, Maxine, Hershie, Heshy, Scarface Louie, Spotty Dave. Julius was teased a lot for being "the genius," but respected, too, and protected by ruffians from ruffians on neighboring blocks. As the kids would not call Einstein "Al," neither would they call our boy "Julie." He was, however, called Orange Julius—after the devil logo of the soft-drink stand, the one with its hands cut off at the wrists. When Julius thought about it at all, he imagined it as a Lucifer-like version of his own amniotic banding. But what sort of womb, and what kind of amnion? A big kid told him it was because the devil had been jerking off.

When it was exceptionally hot, some kids stood out near Nathan's, selling Kool-Aid in successful competition. Not Julius Marantz. In one of his first documented series of experiments, he discovered his own secret formula for an Orange Julius–like drink—frozen OJ, watered-down milk, vanilla, and a little bit of sugar—whipped together in his mother Florence's Osterizer, powered via extension cord from a lamppost tapped by his ingenious, daring father. His customer monopoly was quickly established, resented by his peers but quickly shut down by an observant cop, who drank the dregs of the operation now defunct. No tapping lampposts.

"Who set this thing up?"

"I dunno."

Officer Tarantino called the power department to undo the damage.

Forced indoors in the winter, his second series of experiments involved Newton's ability to walk on the ceiling. How? How did he do that?

Julius washed the gecko's feet with water, then with soapy water, then with detergent—all to no effect. Wesson oil—ineffective; shampoo—equally so; Ajax—boom, boom, combining the obstructiveness of sand with the foaming and cleaning power of God knew what, the greatest disappointment of all. Still the gecko managed his adhesive trick.

Phillip, logically and pedagogically correct, suggested that it might be the ceiling and not the gecko that provided the antigravity effect. So Julius and Newton visited the apartments of four of Julius's his friends. The experimental series ended when the irrational Mrs. Heischuber shrieked that Julius was never to come to her house again. Still, he had determined that Newton was competent on at least two other ceilings besides his own. Materials? The gecko adhered to aluminum foil taped up, to sheet metal held upside down, to wood, to plastic, Formica, and cardboard.

And then, finally, success! Newton fell off the bottom of his mother's new iron (cold), coated with Teflon. Every Teflon pot, pan, and appliance was tried. Eureka! Newton would fall off Teflon. All Teflon. Florence said he could make a TV ad for Teflon and make a million dollars.

But Julius was not interested in a million dollars; he was interested in why Newton's feet stuck to everything except Teflon, and why not to Teflon, and how come he was able to unstick his feet when he wanted to take a step. In all these inquiries, Julius was unsuccessful. He tried feeding Newton various foods, including live mealworms, cockroaches, and Jell-O, but all results remained the same. He was unsuccessful. Unsuccessful. Unsuccessful.

> *Gravity is the evil which drags down and cloys the human soul; it can be both an oppressive and a repressive force. Grace is the opposing force of good which makes possible the release and ascent of the soul. When criteria lose sight of wisdom it is the pull of gravity that predominates.*
>
> —SIMONE WEIL

Why was this piece of paper tacked to the side of the bookshelf in Julius's room? Because his father had found it taped up in the men's room at the Parachute Jump one fine Sunday evening, and snagged it for his boy to consider. At least that's what he said.

"I thought it might cheer you up."

But young Julius didn't really get it. Something to do with gravity.

Thomas Wolfe once wrote, "Only the dead know Brooklyn." Whatever was he thinking? It is true that this most populous of New York's boroughs is dotted—no, splotched—with cemeteries, but surely the inhabitants are not its ultimate connoisseurs. Death was not at all the tone of Julius Marantz's growing up in Coney Island. Not death but life. Mostly he'd had a hell of a time.

For one thing, you could lie out on the beach at night, grabbing tightly onto the sand so as not to fly into space and be ravished by stars. A piece of graffiti on the Stillwell Avenue station declaimed, "DOWN IS OUR ONLY DIRECTION," but Julius understood this as a dubious warning, not a description. He shared his upward preference, he imagined, with the great red flying horse on the gas station, endlessly tacking against the solar wind. Under the Mobil sign of Pegasus, in Maxie's Candy Store on Mermaid Avenue, Julius would read ten comic books for each one he bought, while Max made book in back. In the 1950s it was the only place Phillip could still buy the *Daily Worker.*

Home was on West Thirty-third, near Surf Avenue, close enough to the Italian border at Twenty-fifth to be ever-threatened, but deep enough in the Jewish interior to feel safe, if insular. Eight blocks away, Carmine Mancuso, cigarette pack in his rolled-up t-shirt sleeve, made out with girls and beat up boys who also had muscular arms. But on Thirty-third, arms were not so thick, faces were paler, and bearded men in black shuffled to and from the several tiny shuls of the neighborhood. You never heard of a rape, an assault, or an armed robbery.

The dwellings looked a lot like Woody Allen's settings of his early life—apartment houses of three or four stories, stores on the ground floors—a corner grocery, a tailor shop, a deli, a candy store. There were also smaller, two- or three-family yellow-brick houses, each with a stoop of stairs leading up to a porch.

The Marantzes lived in such a house, in a four-room apartment with its living/dining room, its tiny kitchen, and the parents' and Julius's bedrooms. In the summer, they would take in a boarder who wanted to live near the beach, and Julius would sleep in the living room on the couch. Or on the roof, if it were too hot. Or on the porch. Or in the back yard. Florence might object, but Phillip would insist that "man is an obligate aerobe," and if there were too little air, it was best to try to grab some.

Those summer dog days were spent in the water of hoses and hydrants, or swimming at the beach—water tag and diving for things at the bottom, sunbathing out at the end of the breakwater, limp-sprinting there over the massive, irregular rocks to rest or watch the fishermen. Julius could catch all the crabs he wanted with his hands, but what could you do with a crab? Scare girls? Throw it back.

His swimming skills began with "the dead-man's float" in the several summers' preparation for the rite-of-passage swim out to the third pole. Even skinny Julius could do the dead-man's float in such brine, even "the genius" with his club foot. But even with his new goggles and homemade copper snorkel, all Julius could see was the sunlight glittering sand and miscellaneous debris. He did like pretending to be dead, and was loath to leave off floating for more active pursuits—dog-paddle, breaststroke (that word!), backstroke, and crawl.

On summer evenings, he would roam the boardwalk, watching a world of grown-ups emerge like a nocturnal beast in the change of light. The amusement park flashed gaudiness, and gaudiness became tawdriness, and tawdriness flirted with sleaze, and sleaze with sex. At which point he went home to the twilight pavements and porches of yentas—middle-aged women, stockings rolled down, dresses hiked to cool loose thighs, housewives haunched and humped on chairs and milk crates, spying, talking, tattling.

"How's the genius?" they would ask as Julius made for the stairs.

"Fine." What could he say?

In the house, his undershirted father, nose in *Popular Mechanics* or the *Saturday Review*. "Be glad you're a featherless biped," he once said. "Feathers make you hot."

Initially, it was the biped part that struck him—it was nice that for his father, 1.75 peds counted as two. But Julius often dreamed of feathers, in a nightmarish kind of way—feathers budding from his arm. Scales he could have dealt with. Fur—easy. But feathers . . . what could be as inhuman? Arm feathers. Terrible. More so after hearing from Phillip about Icarus, and reading Auden's poem, and seeing Brueghel's painting on a special trip to the Met, the highlight and endpoint of that minicurriculum.

On the way home, they played Deddy and Icky escaping from the labyrinth, craftsman and apprentice son, inventing improvements for turnstiles and stations and trains.

Icky, being icky, had a question: "Dad, would you drink a glass of your own spit?"

"No," his father said. "Disgusting."

"Why? Don't you swallow it all the time? Let's say I warmed a glass of your spit to mouth temperature . . ."

"Enough."

"Why? What's the difference? You could sip it at the same rate as . . ."

There was no use going further. But the silence from Bay Parkway to Stillwell Avenue suggested they had stumbled on a true mystery, different for grown-up and child, yet springing from the same question: What are my boundaries; where do I end?

But the prime fact of his childhood was the amusement park itself. Freud once dropped in for a look during his brief stint abroad. "Dollaria," he called America, an anti-Paradise governed by ignorant materialism wedded to conformity. Americans, he thought, were anal-retentive sadists, hostile to pleasure but approving of high aggression in business and politics. Coney Island didn't change his opinion. He didn't even ride the rides.

Such was not Childe Julius's take. His was a life of potato chips and pretzels, jelly doughnuts and chocolate bars, halavah, salted peanuts, ice cream, corned beef and hot dogs, salami sandwiches and Dixie cups, consumed in a sprawling, fenced-in fairyland of games and rides, sideshows and food stands, fifteen blocks long and one block wide—from Surf Avenue to the boardwalk. On Tuesday nights, fireworks were shot off a barge at the end of Steeplechase Pier. The four roller coasters were each a rite of passage: the Thunderbolt and the Tornado, the Bobsled and the mighty Cyclone with its electric letters, ten feet high. The Flying Scooters were good, too: the Hi-Ball and the Looper. The Wonder Wheel, yes, and the Parachute Jump.

He learned to drive, or at least to steer, on the electric bumper cars. And his first kid-job, until his mother found out, was walking the Thunderbolt tracks early Saturday mornings, climbing slowly up and down the wooden hills and around the turns. So much lost: keys, glasses, pens, notebooks, dentures, money. He once found a bikini top. Florence was afraid that with his foot, he'd have an accident.

Accidents there were, yes, infrequent, but a formative part of his being. There are some pretty dumb jerks in the world, he knew, fooling around on roller coasters showing off or drunk. Some deaths were likely suicides. Standing up, no hands, in the back? Sitting on the back of the last seat with feet up over the bar? What else could you call it? But accidents, too. A boy from Thirty-fifth Street once drowned. Eliot Weiss fell on a piece of glass and cut an artery. And there were fights, once even a murder, when someone cut in line on a sweltering summer day. The Thirty-third Streeters found the knifing fascinating and unfathomable. Jews didn't do such things.

There was life on the boardwalk, to be sure—but also under it. While older kids explored a sandy sort of semiclandestine sex, Julius's project was digging—digging deep, as deep as he could, deeper than anyone had ever dug; down, down for weeks and weeks, digging toward hell or the antipodes, halfway to the center of the earth. Until Phillip brought a ladder, he had to be extracted with Arnie Perlman's rope. Florence worried about hanging.

She worried a lot. It was nice to have a friendly, concerned mom, overseeing from the windowsill during punchball or tag or roller skating. Nice, that is, until her yelled warnings, and the teasing that followed. Had he hung around Thirty-third Street, Freud would have had a ball.

Florence worried about Julius's stair-versus-elevator races, his relativity experiments, his taking out the garbage all at once. She worried about his practice of running up walls. "What are you, a fly?" she would ask. "You think you're Newton?" She worried about him sleeping out on the fire escape on hot, muggy nights, or even on the roof. She worried about his riding the coaster "just to cool off" and about his going off to spend a Saturday with the "I Cash

Clothes" man. She detested his favorite time, the summer, when streets were constantly filled with the littering and rowdiness of strangers, and noise, often late into the night. Did she want him to spend all his time alone in the public library, reading books in Yiddish? Or staying home, listening to QXR?

His father, on the other hand, seemed to worry about little except, say, why Coney Island was called an island—and he interfered with nothing. As far as Julius was concerned, he was the perfect dad.

It was Florence, however, who always put his "tomorrow's" clothes on the steam radiator so they'd be warm on cold winter mornings. She once bought him a huge bag of marbled immys, the envy of the gang, and when the Duncan yo-yo expert came, she gave him money for a special one, with jewels, and he'd learned tricks especially for her.

6.

Now I Am a Man

When Julius was almost nine, Phillip Marantz went into a booth at New Luna Park, put twelve quarters into a slot, and came out twenty minutes later with a long-playing record for his son. *"Hi, boy. This is your father, and this is my story . . ."*

It was a story of a classical German childhood.

"You think you have it bad in second grade? When our teacher came in, we all had to stand and say, 'Salve, Magister,' and he would say back 'Salvete, discipuli,' even though we didn't talk Latin."

It was a story of the '30s and the marginalization of his family's life. Father told son about the rupture of his studies and his slave-like, secret apprenticeship, about his forced new sense of Jewishness, about Kristallnacht. He narrated the visa adventures, and the trip to America, and his meeting Julius's mother at the Automat through an open pie-compartment. Julius would hear about the war, about Phillip's return to Europe as a GI interpreter, about arresting those who had arrested his own father, about his opening Philip's Phixit, and marrying Florence, and . . . *"I love my little genius boychik and wish you a very happy ninth birthday with many happy returns. This is your father, Phillip, signing off."*

Perhaps as a result of this gift, a sense of his deepening story, at the age of nine, Julius decided to put away childish things. This was a youth born to wear a pocket protector. His interests became less exclusively centered on Thirty-third Street, and as he walked to and from school each day he elaborated plans to secede from puerile reality and enter other epochs, other worlds.

Let us review some of his activities.

Science

Being one-footed, he didn't do sports with the others. The punchball games on the block, the stickball games, and touch football on the beach, with cars and sewers as bases and goalposts—these he watched, and less and less. He did collect baseball cards, and tried to develop a science of flipping to heads or tails at will. But the variables were too great, he realized, and he developed his own early version of chaos theory. He was, however, the best runner up walls, and demonstrated remarkable endurance in his hikes along the beach in spite of his stumping along behind the rest. Strangely, and perhaps exceptionally, he was given a pass by the neighborhood kids, his deformity, according to them, accounting for his smartness, the net result being positive.

It was his thinking and feeling that were expanding. Phillip was astounded when Julius proposed the following during a stroll on the boardwalk: "Dad, how can we figure the height of the Parachute Jump?"

"Maybe ask the guys in the booth."

"How do we know *they* know? I mean, if we wanted to measure it ourselves."

Phillip thought this might be the teaching moment for some elementary trigonometry.

"If we got hold of a transit," he gestured what a transit was, "we could measure the angle up to the top, and . . ."

"But without a transit. Just a ruler."

Phillip realized this was not just a discussion but a trap.

"I dunno. I give up."

"We measure its shadow along the boardwalk just when my shadow equals my height."

That's my boy, Phillip thought, and bought him a large frozen custard with sprinkles.

Julius won two science fairs in school, the first by displaying his mother's appendix in a jar—which Florence had been motherly enough to need excised, and Dr. Sobel had been accommodating enough to pickle. With the jar, gussied up as if it were a religious relic of the first order—the prepuce of baby Jesus, for example—Julius provided an exquisitely rendered copy of a Vesalian intestinal drawing and a short speculation on the evolutionary function of now-vestigial organs.

His second winning entry was more interactive and more questionable, a response to a most traumatic experience. The Gyro was a new kind of Ferris wheel, just open, with cages in which you sat and a lever you could pull to cause your capsule to spin and turn you head over heels while the wheel took you up and around and down. One could lock it for the normal ride, but a bored little rat-toothed attendant didn't bother to tell them a damn thing, so when Ershky, Spooky, and Julius started tumbling they all thought something had gone dreadfully wrong and they were about to die. When they stumbled out, Ershky kissed the ground, but old rat-tooth looked as bored as before.

Sweet, though, are the uses of adversity. A rotating cage, a timer, a simple maze, and four hamsters enabled parents and peers to hold two for controls while observing the effect of vestibular storms (diagram and explanation) on a random selection of these poor small mammals, an experiment that would not have passed current cruelty standards. It earned Julius a blue ribbon, nonetheless.

But it was not physiology that really inspired Julius or satisfied his hunger for the outer reaches of space and time. The night sky, of course, continued to inspire; his reading, too, with Phillip, of Gardner's *Relativity for the Million;* and, strangely, most of all, the two little Scotties, black and white, mounted on tiny magnets, bought from the red-haired, kilted clown with strong white teeth who had sold him

Newton. They'd come together to kiss, all right, but to sniff under tail—no way. No way could he push them close. His friends thought it just a neato novelty, about as significant as a hand buzzer. But Julius understood that something profound was going on, something too large for Science Fair, some real distortion of space-time or energy he could hold right there in his hands. That he couldn't see the lines of force was maddening. What was there? What was keeping them apart in one direction and not another? Magnetic poles, as Phillip averred? That begged the question. Forces, forces. F = ma, at home and at large. The vacant, massy sky above and the repulsion and attraction in his hand. His vector toward physics was assured.

Love, Death, and Sex

They were all interwoven for Julius, even early on. The three horsemen of the apocalypse.

At twelve, Julius got propositioned: he was accosted on the boardwalk by a weird older girl, Jocelyn Hines. She was fourteen or fifteen, he thought, pimpled, heavyish. She had noted his foot and told him he was beautiful, like Byron. Byron who? Julius wanted to know. She tried to touch him, but he pulled away. She said to him:

> Alas! the love of Women! it is known
> To be a lovely and a fearful thing.

Again she tried to touch him, and he pulled away again.

She said:

And their revenge is as the tiger's spring,
Deadly and quick, and crushing; yet, as real
Torture is theirs—what they inflict, they feel.

She asked him to come under the boardwalk with her, but, not knowing what he was getting into, he refused. Besides, she looked a little like his mother.

Six months after this effusion, Jocelyn died of a burst appendix, the second girl he knew to have done so. The horsemen continued to advance.

At twelve, he got pubic hairs, et cetera, and with his friends made a "social and athletic club" in the cellar of an apartment building on Mermaid Avenue near Happy's Luncheonette, the building which also housed Sammy the Pig's pool hall. It was in this underground that an archetypal agon was played out.

Henry Weisbrot was the super's son, not an original member of the Mermen SAC, as indeed his noncircumcision alone would have attested, but a member de facto: it was in the dingy space outside his basement apartment door that social and athletic activities were carried out. He was German, a blond-haired, blue-eyed Aryan of the first order, square-jawed, muscular, and fresh. Henry already owned the full set of weights the club was planning to purchase, and worked out, too, with a punching bag he had set up in a corner of one of the club's two rooms. He was by far the best-looking of the crew, the one that all ten males and one female would have voted as most likely to succeed in losing his virginity and snatching that of others.

That lone female was Maxine Moravics, pronounced Moravitz, a cookie tough enough to be chewed out by ten guys for hanging around, and soft enough, at least under her untucked flannel shirt, to be desired by all. She was as good as Jewish jailbait comes.

The street play of the past was not conducive to hanky-pank, but now that the gang had moved underground, and now that the back room had been furnished with a latch, a mattress, and a candle, the rules had changed, and anything was possible. Not really anything—something. The only questions that remained were when and with whom, and it was the latter that took tremolo-ing precedence.

A Martian, after spending five minutes among the group, would have been able to predict the obvious: Maxine and Henry. All the guys were resigned, and Maxine herself knew the script she had been given. Furthermore, IQ aside, she found him most attractive. But a funny thing happened during the slow dance to the mattress.

Julius began to quote Byron at her, *Childe Harold* and *Don Juan*. Little did he predict that Maxine, an unlikely consumer of poetry, would be so affected that she would begin to be wary of her attraction to the glitter of Henry and his muscles and his sparkling teeth, or the compelling atmospherics of the overheated rooms.

What men call gallantry, and gods adultery,
Is much more common where the climate's sultry,

Julius quoted at her, and

Maidens, like moths, are ever caught by glare,
And Mammon wins his way where seraphs might despair.

And shortly one quite pubescent girl found herself entangled in the surprised embrace of one barely pubescent boy, in a display of psyche over soma dazzling in its unexpectedness. Julius had won a contest he hadn't even entered; he found it pretty nice. The guys were impressed, too. For one thing, it was the Jews' revenge on the Germans.

Not a week later, glowing perhaps with mental sexual energy, Julius was approached by a slim young man outside a boardwalk bathhouse. He didn't know that the volume of Proust he was carrying was a classic signal of sexual orientation. It never rains but it pours. Julius said, "No thank you," and left.

Religion

Given his impressionable Miltonic childhood, it is understandable that Julius might be religiously different from other children in his cohort. For his fourth birthday, Phillip and Florence had bought their "genius boychik" a blue bodysuit with red overbriefs, a red cape, and a big red "S" on the chest, inscribed in a yellow field. It was clear to them that he loved his present, for he immediately climbed up on his bedroom chest and flopped down repeatedly onto his bed. Over the next days it gradually dawned on them that he was making no effort to fly onto his bed, arms outstretched, in classical non-Icarian form. There was no accompanying "Up, up, and away!" as might have been expected in a truly echt performance. To Phillip's offhand inquiry, young Julius patiently explained that Satan didn't say "Up, up, and away." He didn't fly; he fell. Julius was practicing falling—in his Satan suit. Sorting this all out took parental guidance and several DC comic books, which, until then, had not been allowed in the house.

The boychik's next religion, related to the one now banned, was to worship the Imp of the Perverse, another bedtime chicken come home to roost. Poe's Imp was a little creature of the brain who impelled one to approach ever nearer the edge of the cliff, though it might be dangerous or fatal. It might even call on one to jump, just because one knew one shouldn't. Julius was again practicing falling—this time intentionally, not expelled from heaven but rather choosing the irrational just because. Though it was not actually the Imp that was falling, Julius felt it was richest to practice in full Imp regalia, cause and caused at once. Naked except for Superman briefs, his face and hands blackened with burnt cork, S&H green stamps pasted up and down the length of his arms, Davy Crockett coonskin cap on head, fully grimaced and totally angled, he gave out such frightening shrieks that Florence inevitably stopped the ritual, after all that preparation.

Faced with parental resistance, Julius's active religious quest went into hibernation while he pursued less active practice. He meditated long on being made in God's image (another bedtime seed) and its consequences. God was a guy, that much he knew, an old guy—so God's hair, unlike his own, was probably white, and, also unlike himself, He probably had a beard. But there the dissimilarities might end. God had five fingers on each hand, for sure, but did he have a tushy? A peeney? If he did, did he use them to go to the bathroom? Did he get diarrhea? There was something about this strain of inquiry that made Julius reluctant to consult his parents.

When he was nine, in the course of putting away childish things, Julius demanded to go to Hebrew school, like the other kids. Phillip, being of assimilated parents, had not been bar mitzvahed; it was not until the persecution that he had begun to understand himself as a Jew. Julius was too young for bar mitzvah classes. Still, a genius should know Hebrew, Phillip thought. So he enrolled his son at the yellow-brick synagogue on Mermaid Avenue, and, as might have been expected, Julius excelled in the study of that ancient, holy tongue. When he wanted to quit because of the other kids' cutting up, and so he could spend more time practicing for his piano lessons with Mrs. Lobkowitz, Phillip discouraged him. "Shoulders are from God," he said, "and burdens, too."

Julius once went with his family to a wedding in a Christian church. He thought it was boring because the service was in English. What wasn't boring was the spiral staircase built into a wall in the back, leading to the dome above. The treads were acute triangles, and the passage so narrow he had to climb sideways with his back against the wall. He watched the service from the high clerestory of the dome. The bride and groom looked like the figures on their wedding cake, and the organ sounded great.

Two Mitzvahs

Twelve-year-old Julius's first planned religious event was the Bark Mitzvah he threw for Yenta, his cocker spaniel. First came the calculations. At seven canine years per human year, the service must occur at 13 years times 365 days plus 3 (the number of leap-year extra days), all divided by 7. Thus, Yenta might become a dog (as opposed to a puppy) when she was approximately 678.3 days old, or 1.86 years. The event was announced for a Saturday in May, a month and a half before Yenta's second birthday, the first, last, and only Bark Mitzvah ever held on Thirty-third Street. "Thirteen year-equivalents of hair, drool, and droppings," the mimeographed flyer announced. "Service by Julius Marantz. Reception food by Purina. Music by Dogmenico Scarlatti."

Julius held forth in the flowered and crepe-papered cellar of the-Mermen SAC, to twenty friends and slightly fewer parents. The back-room mattress had been stowed that day and replaced by a reading chair and a table covered with *Saturday Evening Posts*. The event was introduced as one of sorrow and yet of joy, Julius being ashamed to relate that in biblical times dogs had had no owners and were considered only nuisances and street scavengers who might even devour human flesh. Rotting meat could be thrown to dogs (Exodus 22:31), and male prostitutes and gentiles were often so described. Even Rabbi Jesus had warned his flock neither to give what is holy to dogs nor to cast pearls before swine, the two unclean animals being equated.

Happily, things had changed, Julius noted, his demeanor brightening. "Just look at our bark mitzvah, Yenta." And here, Danny the Bull came out with Yenta ensconced on a pillow stuffed with bark from the Cedars of Lebanon, Yenta wearing a tiny tallis, Thomas Tallis yclept, and a Brooklyn Dodgers yarmulke pinned to her curly black hair. She immediately leapt out into the crowd and began sniffing crotches, thus demonstrating the origin of her name, and gave out several midrange "ruf!"s, which Julius was quick to point out spelled "fur" backward, the brilliant animal.

Before the service could begin, the problem of Yenta's origins had to be dealt with. She was a stray from the ASPCA, with parents unknown. Was Yenta Jewish?—that was the key question. Since that could not be definitively determined, and since it would be better to be safe than sorry, Julius began with a short ritual of conversion. As he sprinkled both Yenta and her Purina chow with Manischewitz, he recited a verse from Isaiah: *And God will say, make a path, clear the way, remove the stumbling block out of the way of My people.* With Yenta's first bite, the deed was done, the miracle made *(Baruch Atah Adonai Elohenu Melech Ha-olam Boh-Ray P'ree Hagfen),* and Julius proceeded to read what was said to be Yenta's dictated bark mitzvah speech, but which was actually an abridgement of Kafka's "Investigations of a Dog"— which left the congregation quite confused. Nevertheless, the tenor of the event overcame both the need for intellectual coherence and the hint of spiritual desecration, and all joined hands for a spirited hora as Julius banged out some simple Scarlatti on a toy piano borrowed from Ershky Lobkowitz. My son, the rabbi! his parents thought.

But the whiff of sacrilege was not so easily ignored at Julius's own coming of age.

A month before his bar mitzvah in January of 1961, Simon and Yvette Barenboim, refugees from Vichy, and Thirtieth Street friends of Mrs. Lobkowitz, invited her star pupil to a concert of French organ music at the Church of the Ascension, in Manhattan. "Sure," said his parents, "why not?"

This was why not: the organ is not a healthy thing for a good Jewish boy. It knows no limit or restraint. Julius had a guest's distant sense of such immensity during the smaller pieces by Guilan, Daquin, LeBègue, and Duruflé. But the major work of the evening took him through the gates and sprawled him prostrate in the most interior grand hall of Christendom. Jewish music does not presume to utter or describe the holy name. Jewish music is humble. Messiaen's *L'Ascension: Quatre Méditations Symphoniques pour Orgue* is not.

For almost half an hour, Julius was bathed in a sound-world of ecstasy, culminating in the "Prayer of Christ Ascending Toward his Father." Closely massed seraphic sounds, slow, chromatic ascensions to heights of unresolved, sweet dissonance. This is not the world anymore, he thought, bird of spirit that he felt, flown from time into eternity.

Soft cascades of blue-orange chords enveloped him—saturated, radiant colors almost blinding to the ear; the desire for light, for stars; sweet, opulent, voluptuous sound in a world of tonal ubiquity, vastly open to other modes of experience; a universe of infinite time, infinite extent, and infinite power. An exit from the amusement park, at least, a ticket out, thought Julius, a step through the looking glass: the trick is to be unborn.

All this in the context of earlier movements: "Serene Alleluias of a Soul Desiring Heaven," "Transports of Joy of a Soul Before the Glory of Christ, Who Is His Own." Other music's allusive conversations with God seemed utterly superficial. Messiaen was not healthy for a good Jewish boy.

Perhaps it was the Imp of the Perverse which made him do it, this bar mitzvah, this Julius Marantz, son of the commandment. Family and friends gathered at the Temple Beth Israel on Mermaid Avenue, along with congregation members curious to see what the "genius whose parents don't even bother to come to synagogue" would come up with for a performance. They were well-rewarded for their pains.

It was a Saturday service. Julius, because of his long-standing mastery of Hebrew and his general intelligence, was given more responsibility for conducting the service than any bar mitzvah boy in the history of the congregation. A beaming Rabbi Chasen led him up the aisle, tallis over young shoulders, his cousins waving, Julius gangly-stately in a Jewish way, an instar of the new man he had become.

"Baruch atta Adonai," Julius began. *"Eloheynu Melech ha-olam, asher kid-a-sha-nu be-mitz-voh-tav v'tzi-vah-nu la-he-ta-tayf B-tz't-tz't.* Blessed be Thou, God, King of the Universe, who directs us to wrap ourselves in the fringed fabric of the tallis. With deepest gratitude I bless You, whose power governs our mysterious world, for our being sustained, and for our being present at this moment. May the door of the sanctuary of our hearts be wide enough to receive all who hunger for love."

His proud parents, green and nervous at actually synagoguing, gave him their Talmud blessing, read from the floor by Phillip: "Our dearest son, may you live each day to the fullest. May you get the most from each hour, each day and each age of your life. Then you can look forward with confidence and back without regrets. Dare to be different and to follow your star, and don't be afraid to be happy."

Julius's Torah portion, a surprise to Phillip and Florence, was Deuteronomy 21:18–21, which followed unhappily upon:

> 18 *If a man have a stubborn and rebellious son, which will not obey the voice of his father, or the voice of his mother, and that when they have chastened him, will not hearken unto them:*
>
> 19 *Then shall his father and his mother lay hold on him, and bring him out unto the elders of his city, and unto the gate of his place:*
>
> 20 *And they shall say unto the elders of his city, This our son is stubborn and rebellious; he will not obey our voice.*
>
> 21 *And all the men of his city shall stone him with stones, that he die; so shalt thou put away evil from among you, and all Israel shall hear, and fear.*

But Julius seemed inspired by his text. He sought out the knapsack he had stowed at the back of the platform, next to the Ark. From it, while he gave his bar mitzvah address, he slowly pulled twenty stones, gathered from the breakwater, carefully chosen for their shape and handheld heft. He laid the barnacled missiles along the front of the platform, within easy reach of his friends and family.

"We must go straight to the heart of the unacceptable," he began, "if we are to serve the shards of God."

He spoke of the legend of the prodigal son as the story of one who could not stand to be loved. He spoke of all homes as "unsafe houses," potentially annihilating. He spoke of the Jews adopting white for mourning in counterallegory to the rest of the world, and of

Paul's letters to the Hebrews: they never wrote back. Neither did the Corinthians. "According to Pythagoras," he concluded, "we ourselves are the measure of the universe. If this be so," he said, "then pray for us."

The congregation smiled, doubtfully. A pious boy, they hoped.

Julius thanked his teachers and all those who had contributed to his education, including Maxine Moravics. And then he made his announcement: "Jewish visions of God look to the rainbow, to the celestial promise that annihilation will not be visited on created being. Does not this pious hope revoke God's total freedom? I can no longer, in honesty, look through such rainbow-colored glasses. God may condemn us *however* we serve Him: *that* is godly freedom.

"I seek a larger vision than our own, a vision honest enough to admit eternal punishment as a real option for an all-powerful God, beyond good and evil. Today I have become a man, and I will begin my studies toward acceptance into the Roman Catholic Church. *Sholem aleichem, aleichem sholem, omen.* The stones are there to be used."

He removed his tallis and stood there, vulnerable in shirt and tie. It took a moment for the stupefied congregation to connect the Torah reading with his offer. But connect it they finally did. Rabbi Chasen intervened.

"Julius," he said, as if this were mere Talmudic disputation, "conversion is a poisoned chalice. Judaism has always been your home. It has fashioned and shaped your mind, and the very imagination that fancies you can leave. But if you desert us, you will be cut off from your source, from your contact with the world, with your own nature, with the elements that formed you. *That* will be the suffocation you spoke of, that loss of gravity."

Julius, impassive, gathered the stones—all unthrown—back into his knapsack. The public mumble crescendoed to cacophony, and people began to leave the clamorous room.

"Wait, wait!" Rabbi Chasen called out. "There's food, a whole dinner in the community room!" The exodus continued. "You can't waste all this food! There are starving children. . . at least take a doggy-bag!" It was hopeless.

The rabbi watched Phillip Marantz walk slowly from the sanctuary into the banquet hall, scan the pile of presents at the door, and survey the tables with their white cloths and rented glasses. Rabbi Chasen, with Florence Marantz behind him, watched Phillip Marantz pause — and then rush headlong at the gefilte-fish swan crowning the buffet, decapitate it with a slap through its neck, and, with the fury of a two-year-old, scatter chunks of torso all over the floor.

BETH

Faith and Reason

Faith, n. Belief without evidence in what is told by one who speaks without knowledge, of things without parallel.

—AMBROSE BIERCE, *THE DEVIL'S DICTIONARY*

Such words were not for Julius. His thinking at this stage would have been more Nietzschean: "A casual stroll through the lunatic asylum shows that faith does not prove anything." Proof. That was the issue. He had become a scientist, a young man committed to induction, observation, and the drawing of conclusions.

And yet he was on a religious quest. So what, then, was the questing beast for this rational young man; what was the object of his search?

In a thoughtful attempt to undo the Messiaenic damage they sensed they had done, the Barenboims invited Julius to their apartment one night to listen to their first purchase from Sam Goody's, the new Columbia LP recording of Schoenberg's *Moses und Aron.* It proved to be disastrous.

Now, the Talmud asserts that with faith there are no questions, but without faith, there are no answers. Canny enough. But for Julius, Moses' faith led to more questions than ever. If God was truly "single, infinite, omnipresent, unperceived and unrepresentable," as Moses observes, how would he, a mere "now I am a man," ever come to know Him?

Julius left the listening session mentally collapsed, sunk in despair, defeated, as was Moses, convinced now that *all* religious representation, Jewish *or* Christian, was likely to be hopeless, an arbitrary fashioning of images. *"O Wort, du Wort, das mir fehlt!"* Julius, too, needed an authentic Word.

But the vocabulary of science, reason, logic, and clarity seemed too small to contain it. Giving his life up exclusively to reason would mean bidding farewell to his Self forever. If the future were simply that of science, humans might become entirely other, ironically in the image of God—incomprehensible. Should laboratories develop a man with eyes on stalks or seven-league legs, or, for Heaven's sake, a head coming out of his *tuchas,* people might applaud, and find it neither funny nor repulsive! So much for reason—and so much for faith. Both were lacking. It was this doubly compromised path he'd have to tread.

But tread it as the Jew he'd once been, or the Catholic he sought to become? His bar mitzvah speech had been dramatic, yes, but it had been as much theater as true conviction. A great effect, but he could always turn back and be rewarded. The prodigal son.

A Star of Redemption

Franz Rosenzweig had understood *both* Judaism and Christianity as authentic manifestations of one religious truth. For him, both had equally important roles to play, and both would disappear together at the end of time.

Judaism was the fire, the eternal *life;* Christianity was its rays—the eternal *way*. Judaism was already one with God the Father, while the role of the Christian was to preach, to convert, to turn the nations to Him through His son. Judaism's sole task was to survive outside of History, to continue to *be;* Christianity's great triumph was to *do*.

Rabbi Chasen had given Julius Rosenzweig's dangerous book, had waived its temptation, fully expecting his star pupil to affirm his roots with heightened strength. But the bar mitzvah boy bit on the wrong hook. He accepted Rosenzweig's characterization of Christianity, yes, active, triumphant, but entirely rejected his notion of Eternal Judaism.

It was obvious to Julius that "the chosen people" no longer existed, if they ever had. Israel's time as the people of the Bible was past. It was now a nation like unto other nations, inserted back in history, speaking once-holy Hebrew in the marketplace, wholly different from the Zion of old.

The Hebrew Bible had lost its meaning for the church, and thus for the world at large. Christianity now had its own Old Testament, its own books of history. It had its Judges, Kings, and Prophets in its Councils, Popes, and Church Fathers. With Christianity, and with Christianity alone, was the future. If there *was* to be a future, it wouldn't be Jewish.

Judaism was axioms, postulates, theorems—a deductive approach to life. Not for this young scientist. Christianity—and possibly Catholicism—was experimentation, adaptation, observation, induction. The practical science of love.

Which should he choose? The past pulled against the future, but in that cloud of friction, a thirteen-year-old Julius sensed the blurred outlines of a pure vision.

7.

And Thou Shalt Carry Me out of Egypt

The last two sections of our family album contain no photos.

The synagogue cats got the gefilte fish, the rabbi the pickled herring—and then there was silence. The bar mitzvah sat, unmentionable, in the neighborhood's psychic corner, like a deformed, autistic child. Julius was, whether they liked it or not, a man.

The child, however, is father of the man, and Julius's natural piety bound his just-teen days with thoughts like these:

(from his diary, 13 August 1962)

I get it now. The Good Humor men. I know who they are.

They are a secret society of tsaddikim, trying to teach the world from the boardwalk. They ring their prayer bells and serve up the body and blood of the Eternal in little Dixie cups.

Dixie cups are not from the South. They were invented in Boston. I looked it up. Now they make them in Pennsylvania. So they must get their name from "dixit," *"it is spoken," intensely spoken.*

You hold the cup in your hand, you feel its coolness, and with the other hand, you struggle to control the little wooden spoon while prying loose the tab to lift the cover.

Open ye heavens, and behold! Underside, there it is—the universal mystery, the great yin/yang of complementary opposites—chocolate and vanilla. And under the brown and white—lick them off, it's OK to lick—lies yet another mystery. O tsaddikim, how crafty you are! A layer of waxed paper—but not the ordinary waxed paper Mom wraps cream-cheese-and-tomato sandwiches in—a special waxed paper, thicker, found nowhere else in the universe probably—under this layer, semiopaque, lies an image, hard to see. Blue of the beyond, the mountain's foggy mists—someone, something, is under there.

Now comes the moment of joy, religious ecstasy, known perhaps to Saint Teresa, I would think: using the waxed-paper tab, you s l o w l y peeeeel away the barrier. Not too fast, keep it coming, now . . . And lo and behold—a face, blue as Krishna's. It's Bobby Darin, or Paul Anka, or Annette Funicello, clear and luminous, our current stand-ins for gods and goddesses.

But it isn't the existence of the face that is so impressive (though we "collect" them). It is the revealing of the face—the lesson that behind the everyday world, beneath and beyond even its most delicious brown-and-whiteness, there lies still another—the world of the gods, a world that can be glimpsed by peeling away, peeling away. . . .

If that isn't good humor, what is?

Correction: the child is *one* father of the man. There was another father, too. As Julius was growing up, Phillip Marantz was growing down—or in, or out, or around—in any case, what Florence thought of as "more childish."

He cried a lot in those days—cried at music, cried when he tried to read beautiful things aloud, cried, even, at the thought of the word "big." Those were the good tears. But he cried, too, at the new housing projects, eating the parks away. He cried at the closing of stores on Mermaid Avenue, at any shop boarded up on Surf. First a cleaner was gone, then a TV repair, then a shoe store, then one of the delis. Where would people shop? He cried because the beaches were getting dirtier, the roller coasters more bedraggled, the bad places worse.

It was once the rich who were his enemies; now it was also the poor, the welfare families dumped into Sea Gate, the drugs, the violence and vandalism, the muggers and rapists. New, new, new. Bad, bad, bad. City planners who would improve the place out of existence, neighborhoods being torn up . . . anger and tears.

"Grow up," advised his wife.

"Up," he thought. "The crisis of up versus down."

Of that Phillip there were no photos.

He haunted the library, reading the Greeks. "The road uphill and the road downhill are one and the same," his Heraclitus said. And in Aristophanes, the creation of birds from the mating of Chaos and Eros. Birds, first among living creatures. Daedalus wing-buds itched near his scapulae. He rubbed his back against his chair.

Never really Jewish before, he would now say a *brucha* before reading certain authors—Peretz, Singer, Sholem Aleichem, even the archgoy Robert Frost:

> Why make so much of fragmentary blue
> In here and there a bird, or butterfly,
> Or flower, or wearing-stone, or pen eye,
> When heaven presents in sheets the solid hue?

He spoke a lot of *musar*—an untranslatable Hebrew word—Jewish humanism, transcendentalism, growth, and possible holiness all in one. He noted that the tail gunner on the *Enola Gay* had worn a Brooklyn Dodgers cap. On the day of JFK's assassination, it was the death of Aldous Huxley that moved him to tears.

Two Novembers later, when the Northeast power grid failed and the lights went out from New York City to Boston and west all the way to Toronto, the new neighborhood became the old again: in the darkness, strangers emerged, not as shadows but far more substantial than usual, child-like, laughing with flashlights and candles, helping, holding hands, carrying things off with gorgeous merriment. Phillip felt healed, and hoped the current would not come on again.

It was too dark for photos.

He told Julius for the umpteenth time about the great snowstorm of '47, which had greeted his birth into the world with similar friendliness. He joked again—about the cows shot into space, the herd shot 'round the world—a fourth grade joke. But they laughed together again, and came together again, and went to the planetarium again, and were thrilled together, midwinter, at the emergence of the stars.

And Phillip became interested in pyramids. It was the '60s: the New Age had begun, even in Coney Island, and Pyramid Power was nascent in the air. *Because we were slaves unto Pharaoh in Egypt* . . . even a Jew, especially a Jew, might get involved. Phillip joked about saving money on razor blades but was more serious about experimenting with containers the exact proportions of Gizeh to keep milk indefinitely fresh. Experimenting, patenting, manufacturing, and retiring on Easy Street, Coney Island. His initial food-mummification trials with hamburger meat, liver, eggs, and milk versus controls were auspicious, and he was hot to visit the real thing, to inspire and inform his own designs.

He began saving for the trip.

Julius joined in the investigation. His experiments included unsuccessful mummification attempts within cones, tetrahedrons, octahedrons, dodecahedrons, icosahedrons, and even a Bucky Fuller dome, just coming into vogue. A hole in the wall didn't do it either. There was something about pyramids. . . .

The Great Pyramid at Gizeh. Its base perimeter was 36,524.24 inches. One terrestrial year is 365.24 days. The sum of base diagonals was 25,827 inches. The precession of the equinox is 25,827 years. Those guys knew more about astronomy than modern science did up to the International Geophysical Year of 1957–1958.

The Marantz pyramids were built on a 72-inch base, were 45.8 inches high, were vented with large holes to maintain equal temperature throughout, and took up all of the back room at Phillip's Phixit. They were constructed from cardboard, wood, plaster, Plexiglas, steel, copper, aluminum, cement, and various combinations. Materials made no difference; it was only the shape that mattered. Cats would sleep in the pyramids by preference; when Julius sat in one, he felt intense heat, and his hands would tingle. The shapes worked best aligned along the earth's magnetic field. Normal razor blades lasted two to three Phillip shaves, pyramid blades two hundred.

Alas, though planned, there were no photos.

Tickets were bought: Phillip and Florence Marantz, 17 December 1966, EgyptAir Flight 988, New York to Cairo. Two weeks later, Julius was at Kennedy to greet their return.

A crowd of people was waiting for the flight on New Year's Eve, now three hours late. Although festive HAPPY NEW YEAR 1967 signs hung everywhere, the gate was pervaded by a postictal, late-night sadness, and the crowd was cranky and impatient. There was only one man at the counter, deflecting inquiries in robot-like fashion.

"Communication with Flight 987 has been temporarily interrupted. You'll have to stand by for further information."

Nineteen-year-old Julius had his eye on a slim young woman pacing at the back of the lounge. When the new year had struck, and the crowd had grumped in celebration, she stomped up to the counter.

"Someone out there has the information. You know perfectly well where this plane is. If you don't tell us right now, I'm going to raise hell."

"I understand your concern, Miss, and I'm trying to get you the most up-to-date. . ." He turned his attention back to his headset.

Julius's heart went out to her for her feistiness in the face of bland, and for her fierce beauty. An hour later, the loudspeaker gave some relief.

"All those awaiting arriving passengers on EgyptAir Flight 987, please proceed to Gate 82A. All those awaiting arriving passengers on EgyptAir Flight 987, please proceed to Gate 82A."

The official listened at his headset and announced, "Flight 987 has made an emergency landing. It's possible there's been some damage to the aircraft, and some passengers may have sustained injury." The crowd veered back to the desk.

"Has anyone been killed?"

The official concentrated on his headset.

"Has anyone been killed?"

"How many have been killed?"

"It's possible there are no survivors," came the word.

The crowd gasped. And Julius: "Oh God. Oh God. Goddammit. Goddammit." He pushed his way to the back of the crowd. "How could this happen? How could this happen?"

The young woman, tears falling quietly, watched Julius also start to cry—and hyperventilate.

"What are you looking at?" he demanded. "What are you *looking* at?"

She stood there, now staring at the carpet and shaking her head. Julius put his arms around her for both their sakes.

There were no photos.

Hours later he spoke to her: "Are you all right? Do you need a ride home?"

"I—I—I—I have a car, but thanks." She seemed doubtful.

"You think you can drive?"

"I think so. Yes."

"Then you give *me* a lift. I don't think I can."

She told him she was Lydia Lenz, and her mother was dead.

They were each other's comfort in the next months, and each other's distress. Newly twenty, he was an aspiring physicist, destined, he vaguely thought, for wealth and fame. At twenty-one, she was an aspiring Catholic Worker, destined, she hoped, to spend her life in self-denial and service to the poor. A common loss of parents in an uncommon accident is enough to initiate a connection, but not necessarily to sustain it. He danced to Eros, she to Agape. Their drummers were distant, and led them soon, and sorrowfully, apart.

Lamentation on the Loss of Jewish Parents

My father was never big on telling jokes. This may be typical of people who suspect life itself is a joke. Nevertheless, he had a few favorites, Jewish jokes, which he told over and over. Here is one:

Mr. and Mrs. Goldberg, both in their nineties, go to see their lawyer.

"What's on your mind?" he asked.

"Ve vant to get a divorce."

"A divorce? Why? You're ninety years old; you've been married for seventy years. Why now?"

Mrs. Goldberg pipes up: "Ve vere vaiting for the children to die."

What my father thought funny about this, I supposed, was the apparent reversal. But I wonder now if he wasn't making an otherwise unspeakable comment about his marriage to my mother. Divorce, after all, is for the goyim. Even in the worst marriage, parents must stay together "for the sake of the children."

Was theirs the worst marriage? If so, they hid it pretty well.

But what about the inverse? Do Jewish children stay alive for the sake of the parents—so as not to disappoint them by dying? Is staying alive part of their never-ending performance requirements? If so, then a Jewish parent's death may be a source of ultimate liberation, devoutly to be wished.

For all my love of my loving parents, my father the teacher, my mother the caretaker, for all my tears at the airport, I shortly found myself pondering the joy of new freedom.

Grief is an unstable thing—far more so for me than it was for Lydia. What was the difference between us? Male/female certainly, but could it also have been Jewish/Catholic?

The world has an image of the breast-beating Jew, always moaning and kvetching, ever bewailing his fate. Yet Rabbi Chasen instructed me well in the Kaddish, that central, punctuating blessing in Jewish prayer. Every Jewish Jew can speak the text by heart, as Christians can the Lord's Prayer.

The mourner's Kaddish: not a word about death or the dead. No acknowledgment whatsoever of grief. Instead, exuberant praise for God. That's it—praise. Things come, and they go. Praise. People die. Praise for their life and its cosmic path. *Magnified and sanctified may His great name be in the world that He created.*

Displacement. It does take the sting out of things.

Several years ago, I was in the Mag Lab thinking of my parents playing with the black-and-white Scotties. I had to hide my tears. A Russian postdoc, Vladimir Somsikov, came up to me and whispered in my ear one of his many Caucasian sayings: "Real men do not cry. Their tears are brought by wind." And up from somewhere in the crannies of my soul blew the roller-coaster wind, the wind of the Parachute Jump. I burst out bawling, all Kaddish suspended.

I see myself here as "a Jewish child." That was then, the then of the past. There is also a then of the future.

But still I lament their passing. I do. Tears brought by many winds.

8.

Taking Flight

"My friends," says Chadband, "Why do we need refreshment, my friends? Because we are but mortal, because we are but sinful, because we are but of the earth, because we are not of the air. Can we fly, my friends? We cannot. Why can we not fly, my friends?"
Mr. Snagsby ventures to observe in a cheerful and rather knowing tone, "No wings." But is immediately frowned down by Mrs. Snagsby.

—CHARLES DICKENS, *BLEAK HOUSE*

Nineteen sixty-eight was a good year for flying. It was a good year to start college. Especially in Denmark. Especially at New Experimental College, the brainchild of a nisseman named Aage Rosendal Nielsen. Cross his Santa with his Imp of Perversity and you'd likely generate his admissions questionnaire. Among normal, Harvardish questions, it asked:

1. What is a question?
22. What do you want the world to be like after you have left it?
23. Where will you be then?
26. Under what circumstances do people scare you?
27. How beautiful is your anger?
31. What is infatuation?
36. How are you god-like?
38. How are you learning to take in your suffering?
47. How sneaky can you be?
49. Why are you such a good person?

Julius's answers convinced Aage they could use him. It was the Hamletness of Denmark that convinced Julius to go. That, plus a letter sent to Coney Island, addressed to Phillip and Florence Marantz, and opened by their orphan:

Dear Parents,

You may be reluctant to see your child at an institution such as ours. Such concern is natural and good, and you do not want your children wasting time or money at a school unhelpful to maturing, to becoming responsible, or for acquiring an education which will help them make a living. I share your concerns.

Most children who have come so far have come

here, rather than to the schools you might prefer, because you have not been good enough parents or because they are better children than you expected them to be. It is likely that your behavior did not match your stated ideals, or that there was a lack of genuine relationship in the family. These are terrible things to subject children to for years on end.

Children are so wonderful and idealistic that if they don't find authentic behavior or genuine relationships in their homes, they will look for them for the rest of their lives, look harder for them than for success as you understand it. As a result of attending NEC, they may reject you and your lives. This will be painful and will require your utmost understanding and support.

One thing I consistently try to do is encourage students to write their parents—and everyone else—in the most open and frank way possible. Sometimes parents respond indignantly, saying that they were good parents, always had a good relationship, always tried to do their best. But you know your best never suffices. If you are lucky enough to have children who can express their discontent and their dreams, then listen to them, be proud of them, and realize how much they are helping you, even if it hurts.

Sincerely yours,

Aage Rosendal Nielsen, Rector

New Experimental College

Skyum Bjerge, 7752 Snedsted, Thy, Danmark

At the end of his first semester, Julius made the following presentation for the approval of the community: "Aage, Sara, Tom, Ruth, John, Pippy, Terri, Kelly, Bill, Jim, Hennig, Mogens, Elmo, Elaine, Jane, Emil, Alan, Doris . . .

"I feel it's important for me to have both definite goals and indefinite ones. The definite ones will be best met at the University of Copenhagen Physics Department, with three full semesters of their normal undergraduate curriculum—mechanics, electromagnetism, thermodynamics, relativity, quantum theory, etc. I have already begun my study in many of these areas and I trust will be able to manage a heavy course load and pass the normal examinations. And during my three residencies here at NEC, I will teach three courses in "Physics for the Inquiring Mind." With this background, I should get into whatever graduate school I choose.

"More important, however, and the reason I came to NEC, is that I wish to develop—and I'm serious—the cardinal and theological virtues: courage and excellence, temperance and justice, faith, hope, and charity. I expect my stay at NEC to lead me in that direction.

"At the moment I am nothing. I am, as Aage says, empty and stupid. I would like to put others before myself, and I'm miserable because I find that hard to do. Sometimes I think crazy things like about joining a motorcycle gang, or what it might be like to sleep with God. Some of my screws may be missing. I want to find them here. So in addition to my career goals, I also want to study a quite indefinite thing, area, cloud, wisp: Julius Marantz.

"I invite you all to instruct me in this subject, in classroom or kitchen or bedroom, in person or in correspondence, during my Copenhagen semesters. I will choose my work-study so as to learn most about myself. I will teach you physics so that we may both discover ourselves in the teaching. Why should learners be left out of the learning? Are we afraid education will become too involving, endless, unfathomable? NEC is the place to extend the variables. Yet I expect nothing from NEC per se. I expect it all from us, especially myself. *Mange tak.*"

His proposal was enthusiastically accepted by the school assembly, the Ting. He went off to Copenhagen for fall semester.

To supplement Phillip and Florence's insurance payments for tuition, room, and board and to pay for his apartment in the city, his home away from home away from home, Julius took a job as relief personal-care attendant for a Karen Lange, three hours a day, seven days a week, to spell Fru Witte, her permanent caretaker. He wondered why a male would be trusted with the personal care of a seventeen-year-old girl. He wondered even more when Fru Witte introduced them.

There, lying in bed, was the most beautiful young woman he had ever seen. Something was indefinably odd about the whole picture, but Karen's huge, intensely blue eyes, her perfect features, set off by long, golden hair, and her charming English made for an inward quivering, a contraction of his viscera, as if to protect himself, to protect his job, or to protect her. He caught his breath, held himself still, and was all business at the interview. But when Fru Witte had left them, the tremolos began again. Until—

"Mr. Marantz, I need to go to the bathroom."

He stood there, helpless and confused.

"I will show you how to help me. Don't be afraid; it's quite easy. I don't weigh much. Take down my covers."

He did so, with trepidation. And then he knew what seemed so odd, and why he was so trusted. Under the covers, wrapped in a cotton shift, was the body of a tiny creature, almost fetal in aspect. A little bird, he thought, still in the egg, not much more than creamy skin encasing miniature bones. Her legs and arms were covered with golden hair, as was her tiny pubis, when revealed. Her nipples protruded from her cage of ribs, with only the slightest suggestion of breast beneath them. Her lower legs were bare, and her feet, if feet they were, were fitted out with socks.

"Take me under my arms and under my legs," she instructed, quite calm.

He did so, rather agitated.

"The bathroom is through that door."

He carried her in and placed her on the toilet, adjusting her clothing appropriately.

"Do you want me to go?" he asked.

"No, no. I'll just be a second."

He had never seen a girl pee. It was less arcane than he had imagined. Quite simple, in fact. Why had he imagined otherwise?

"Please wipe me."

This was more than he'd bargained for, but he made a good show of it, carried her back to bed, and tucked her in.

"There," she said. "That's the worst of it. Now what shall we do for fun?"

They agreed that fun might be teaching each other their respective languages. She was far ahead of him, of course, he being an American. But a year at NEC had given him a good start.

They read Hans Christian Andersen to one another, first he in English, then she in Dansk. He teased her about being a *fattig lille Pige*—a poor little girl—such riotously false cognates. But, ah, *"Der var engang"*—that lovely formula of "Once upon a time." *Der var engang,* once upon a time, a time that has passed, a time when things could be other, *der var engang en Prinds,* a prince, *der var engang en Kone,* a woman. And above all, *der var engang en lille Pige,* a little girl, *saa fin og saa nydelig,* so pretty and so dainty. And her name was Karen.

Saa fin og saa nydelig. That she was the unfortunate dancer of "The Red Shoes" did not matter so much as that her beloved Andersen had written about a Karen, *saa fin og saa nydelig,* a Karen whose mirror had told her, *"Du er meget mere end nydelig, du er delig!"* "You are much more than pretty—you are beautiful"—this she found wonderful. "Once she had begun," he wrote, "her legs continued to dance."

Mine can hardly move.

"Dance you shall," Death said, "dance in your red shoes till you are pale and cold, till your skin shrivels up and you are a skeleton!"

I'm already pale and cold and skeletal—but oh, I can dance, I can dance.

That Andersen's Karen was "forsaken by every one and damned by the angel of God" for her joy in the willful shoes, and that to escape their compulsion, she asked for amputation—so what?

Mine are as good as gone, she thought.

And indeed they were—small, dangling appendages of skin-wrapped bones in thin white socks.

She confessed all her sin, and the executioner struck off her feet with the red shoes; and the shoes danced away with the little feet across the field into the deep forest.

And he carved her a pair of wooden feet and some crutches, and taught her a psalm which is always sung by sinners; she kissed the hand that guided the axe, and went away over the heath—to church, and to her death, her heart so filled with sunshine, peace, and joy that it broke apart, and *her soul flew on the sunbeams to heaven.*

Hmmm. An odd achievement. An odd connection. But this was an odd young girl.

"I can dance in my imagination," the bird-girl argued, and Julius went along.

But as fall turned into winter, her vibration seemed to change. The story she wanted to hear over and over, like a child, was now "Den lille Havfrue," "The Little Mermaid." Yes, the mermaid was *smukkeste af dem allesammen,* the prettiest of all her sisters, with *Hud var saa klar og skjær som et Rosenblad,* skin as bright and pure as a rose petal, and *Øine saa blaa, som den dybeste Sø,* eyes as blue as the deepest lake. And yes, again, she had no operative legs—*Kroppen endte i en Fiskehale,* her body ended in a fish's tail. But that seemed secondary to her siblinghood with the girl in the bed.

Karen seemed focused on the asymmetry of love between the all-sacrificing mermaid and the careless, callous prince. She was subtly peeved, even angry at Julius, as if *he* had gone off and married a princess, or were about to. On Christmas Eve, as they sipped champagne, she watched the bubbles burst and cried. Why? "I cry for the Little Mermaid," she said, "dissolving into foam."

Julius dried her tears with his handkerchief.

“Want to hear a Christmas carol you don’t know?” she asked, not quite brightening.

“Sure,” he said.

“It is words written by Andersen.”

And she sang in a trembling, scarcely audible voice, still on the edge of more tears:

Barn Jesus i en krybbe lå,
skønt Himlen var hans eje.

Julius looked at her, a child curled in her own *krybbe*, the dark sky, her sky, out the window . . .

Men stjernen over huset stod,

Many stars over her little house, too.

og oksen kyssed barnets fod.

Instead of oxen it is me. And I would kiss her little feet.

Halleluja! Halleluja! Barn Jesus!

Tears were quietly streaming down from her lightly shut eyes. She seemed to be pouring out her soul into this little ditty. Julius’s heart convulsed in pity. He took her tiny, cold fingers in his hand. She looked at him, then her eyelids, edged with golden lashes, closed once more and glittered with her tears.

"Will you wipe my eyes again?" she asked.

Julius did so, tenderly.

"In my dreams I am whole, with feet," she said. "But when I wake up and want to run, or swim, or dance, it's as if I were tied up."

"I know," he said.

"Last night, I dreamed I was walking in a field of cornflowers with a big red dog, who was growling and trying to bite me. All the worried flowers turned their heads to watch. Blue, blue, blue."

"Like your eyes," he said.

"I thought I'd pick some, make a garland for my hair. I tried to . . . I tried to pick them, but they melted away in my fingers. Then in the field, I saw a bed, like this one here, but someone else was in it. He cried out, 'Karen, Karen!' Oh, I thought, what a shame I have no crown of flowers. I'll put the moon on instead. So I drew the full moon down from the day sky, and I began to shine and light up the whole field. When I came to the bed, I saw who was there. Jesus. It was Jesus himself. I just knew—I don't know how. He was long and young, and all what I could see was dressed in white. He stretched out his hand to me. 'Do not be afraid,' he said. 'Karen, my bride, come to me in my heavenly mansion, and sing the songs of Paradise.' I took his hand, and he drew me to the bed, and lifted the cover for me to get in. The dog barked and barked, but it had to stay behind, and I realized the dog was my sickness, and that in the kingdom of heaven, I wouldn't be sick."

Julius was moved and afraid.

"*Du,* Julius, will you come in bed with me? I feel so cold. Will you undress and come into bed, so I may have the warm of your body next to me?"

He did not move. He stood and breathed.

"Jeg opfatte," she whispered. He didn't. Understand.

Was he practicing some cardinal or theological virtue with an eye toward the good? Was he putting others before himself—or vice versa? Was he being a cloud or wisp? Whatever was involved, his work-study was self-illuminating. But darkly so.

His last contract day was at year's end. In the time they had left, they read stories about chickens, and pigs, and beetles, and snails. They avoided much. They avoided "The Ice Queen." Julius Marantz never saw Karen Lange again. Nor did he write.

He had missed the annual Christmas bash at NEC—as had half the student body, who used the vacation to travel in Europe or visit back home. Those who remained tried to outdo one another playing nisseman, the mischievous Christmas elf who gives presents but also plays tricks. Chief nisseman, of course, was Aage, who had had the most practice and, being sixty-three, was the most playful, sneaking around 24/5 with his invertebrate goblin gait, doing THINGS. One of the things was to stuff all student stockings with a giant home-baked fortune cookie, within which was his annual Christmas message, tightly folded. It read:

Dear Stupid Student, I like you, but so what? You are well-meaning and idealistic, but so what? You are stupid.

I think you are stupid because you don't take the reins into your own hands. You don't follow through and take over the school, and the world before we old folks give up. You are stupid because you don't use your goodwill and idealism for more than your own shortsighted needs.

You often use my stupidity, or your parents', or the Establishment's as an excuse for your own. Stupid. You need to do better than we did and not use methods and elbowing which are familiar.

You come to me with stars in your eyes, or with your confusions, without getting the benefit from your uncertainties. Don't you see that I demand certainty from you because I myself am uncertain? I expect you to see through my superficial behavior and the way I hold to outdated standards and requirements. You must reject me and develop a deeper search.

OK, so you're stupid. I want you to leave your stupidity here when you leave and find those new forms which will be constant alternatives to the old ones. If you don't do that, you will continue to be stupid.

Nisseman One

While Daedalus had instructed his child not to fly too high, Aage was instructing his children not to fly too low.

How did he know these things? Julius wondered. Had he spoken to Karen?

The following summer, in preparation for his fall semester in Copenhagen, he was admitted to the janitorial staff of the Niels Bohr Institute, the janitorial staff with the highest collective IQ on the planet. An hour a day of emptying wastebaskets, cleaning blackboards, and sweeping in one of the institute's ten buildings and nine underground tunnels, 150 kroner per week plus free-access hobnobbing, rubbing the great elbows of theoretical and experimental physics.

It was there he met Richard Feynman and Greg Boebinger, who would be his graduate and postdoc mentors. He was again a janitor in 1971, and finished up his Copenhagen coursework that fall with highest honors.

His Skyum Bjerge springs were equally rich, though more confusing. At his graduation ceremony, the "misplaced harvest of June 1972," Aage announced: "We confer upon you this Bachelor of Arts degree. Now, go and earn it."

"What does that mean?" Julius asked.

"It means becoming conscious of the life and death projected in each moment," the Rector said.

GIMEL

Excursus on Gravity

You are always hovering above yourself, but the higher ether, the more refined sublimate into which you are vaporized, is the nothing of despair.

—KIERKEGAARD, *EITHER/OR*

What keeps us from rising?

The fallen Martin Heidegger may be of some help. We, he notes, are thrown into existence, not like a pop fly, or even like a good strong peg, but like an old cigarette butt, tossed out God's window, perhaps with half a right foot. *Verfall,* he calls it, a fallenness prior to any corruption in the Garden of Eden. Adam, pre-apple, was already falling by virtue of mere existence.

Torn from its authentic Self, our Being plunges downward into everydayness, into the routine habits and conventions, the idle talk, mere curiosity, and "whateverness" of the "They." We crash like a falling plane into the groundlessness of inauthentic existence, into a world in which everything is already "already," a given world, alienated and scattered far from the possibilities of authentic existence. We find ourselves simply "there," amidst incessant bustle, without knowing where we are from or where we are heading.

Our plunge is hidden by public interpretation, so much so, indeed, that it is understood as "ascending" and "living concretely," and we feel at home in this tranquilized world of everyone, a where not conducive to rising. Thus sayeth the Rector.

But this is only the beginning, for from such a fall comes Angst. And on this amusing topic, whom better to consult with than Søren Kierkegaard, the most melancholy of the four great Danes in Julius's life?

As we become addicted to the world, we become unable to free ourselves from its pull. "Thought," Kierkegaard wrote, "becomes so heavy that no wingbeat can lift it up into the ether. If it moves, it sweeps along the ground like the low flight of birds when a thunderstorm approaches." We are attracted thus to what we fear, the Imp of Perversity now ubiquitous. Julius, you, your author here, *anyone* struggling to lead a good and true life—anyone who confronts the abyss of sinful inauthenticity can here become dizzy, and fall, and in falling become dizzy once more in a devil's circle again most unconducive to rising. We psychically grab onto what we can; we cleave to our Angst; we choose powerlessness and lose our focus on ultimate concern. Rising becomes out of the question.

The more profound we are, the graver the danger of falling. So many issues threaten our equilibrium: while Angst presupposes our desire for the good, and suggests the possibility of freedom, this freedom itself, this call from outside the trap, this alone makes us dizzy with unrealized possibility. But if we escape, we meet the Great *Un*truth, the biggest lie of all—the maddening unreliability of "knowledge." Angst is the last stop before transgression, a well-trodden path. Our culture of Angst leads downward.

How far down can we go? Camus writes, "There is only one truly serious philosophical problem, and that is suicide." Imagine being continuously weighted with that thought. Imagine being so heavy, so full of self, as to need to destroy that self, to crush it under Sisyphus's heavier boulder.

Founder, then, o humans, in your tense sea of humility. Live out the Parable of the Jell-O—slogging, weighted down, through dark red slurry embedded in bone. Black cherry is the Fruit of Paradise: if you turn your heads, you may observe its amniotic light outside the bloodstained windows. *Flores, flores para los muertos.*

From Being per se, through the flagellations of the psyche, via the fathers, and their oppressions, and their "cleansing" religions—thus downward forces do inform against us, weighing down our wings, heavying the water of our lives, and keeping us from rising.

• • •

The Czech writer Bohumil Hrabal confessed that his worldview had been formed by a warning he had once been given by a dry cleaner in Prague: "Some stains can be removed only by the destruction of the material itself."

9.

Alumni News

So much for the scrapbook, now just scraps. Snapshots fade and tear, and a family album, though still precious, loses weight when family no longer exists. Julius was henceforth on the lam.

No more Coney Island, no more Skyum Bjerge. No more Mom and no more Dad, no more Nisseman. And worst of all, no more Lydia.

Under such circumstances, we try to maintain connection, but too often there is no one at the other end.

To wit:

1661 Tenth Ave.
Brooklyn, NY 11215
USA
6 September 1974

Hej Aage,

Progress report from NEC's first wayward physicist, now competing for Sneakiest Alumnus Award. My first (meta)physics gig. You may have read about this last month, but probably not about my role.

Remember my telling the Ting about the juggler I met in Christiania, the "I am wild like a wolf" man? I bumped into him in New York about six months ago, juggling in Washington Square, and he got into a flamboyant rave about wanting to tight-rope walk across from one building of the World Trade Center to the other. When he heard I was in physics and had studied engineering and astronomy, he sank his wolf teeth in, and wouldn't let go—would I help him figure and set up the rigging? It turned out he was the guy who did the guerrilla tight-rope walk between the Notre Dame towers in '71.

Needless to say, I was suckered in to help him plan and execute a "clandestine walk," 110 stories up, a quarter mile in the air. Sure, why not? The spirit of NEC.

Philippe (Petit) is a really nice guy—twenty-five going on four, I'd say. A wolf-child, for sure. "I cannot go for long without visiting the vastness of the sky," he told me, and "A man conscious of his death approaches perfection." When I reminded him that he could really be killed, especially given the winds up there, he said, "What could be better than a happy man in flight, in midair?" In short, a nut. But an inspiring one.

The high wire seems to be his life, his oxygen in "the kingdom of the void." He talks about it with stars, galaxies, in his eyes: "the soul of the wire," "the song of the cable," "the time of the rope," "a line pulled tight by the strength of your eyes," "a terrain bounded by death." He thinks of himself as "an air angel come to earth." "I will become the emperor of the American sky."

Well, we walked around at the construction site like tourists. But we needed to get up to the top to determine the anchor points. So using Aage Nielsen-type stealth, we forged some foreign-looking ID and pretended to be architectural reviewers from *Arkitekten-DK*—and we actually got the grand tour from the project office, to the top, everywhere. We asked all kinds of questions. Took pictures. Amazing what French brashness plus NEC training can do. When we got down again, he said, "The towers belong to me. No one can take this away from me. It is impossible, but I know I'll do it." We got together in Philippe's East Village sublet to plot.

Problem One—how to gain access to the buildings. How could we bring a team of people, at least four, and all the equipment—the wire, the hardware, the winch, etc.? We figured some kind of forged worker's pass, and then equipment up the freight elevator, stashed on a high floor among the heaps of construction materials.

Problem Two—how to rig the cable. We had to find footings along the edges of the buildings, since rigging from the central beams would add another three hundred pounds of wire. And the guy wires to prevent side sway—how would they work? You normally attach guy wires to ground, optimally at 45 degrees. The ground is too far. The windows don't open. No place to attach. So we'd have to make the guy wires practically horizontal to the main wire, and far less stable. We could use a bow and arrow to shoot a fishline across from one tower to the other, eighteen-pound test, attached to forty-four-pound test, then parachute cord, and finally a three-eighths-inch nylon rope. We could drag the cable across on that.

But the wind was a serious worry. A pilot friend warned that the turbulence between the two towers could be severe and completely unpredictable. And what if the buildings swayed? If the towers moved, the tension on the wire could increase from five tons to a thousand tons, and snap it—with Philippe on it. I tried to get him to reconsider. Guess what he said. "There are only two solutions in my mind—to do it or to kill myself." QED. He goes back to France to pick up equipment and two friends he had worked with on Notre Dame, Jean-François Heckel, a math teacher, and Jean-Louis Blondeau, a photographer.

OK, here we go, then, the four of us. 6 August, Hiroshima Day, the spirit of death still in the air. We rented a van and drove to the WTC, directly down the access ramps to the underground loading platform. The main cable—200 feet, seven-eighths-inch thick, 270 pounds—was packed into a large wooden box on a dolly. A wheeled suitcase contained the fittings, clamps and tools. Philippe's balancing rod had been jointed in four places and looked like tubing. We were all dressed in work clothes and hard hats, and hot to trot—but we had to wait an hour for a free elevator.

We got out on the 104th floor of the South Tower with the equipment, divided the coil into four parts, and each of us hoisted sixty-eight pounds of it up a stairway that led up four more flights. We must have looked official—we passed lots of workers, and no one said a thing. Up a final stairway to the roof. We parked our stuff Purloined Letter style, out in the open, among the other construction materials. At about 4:30, Jean-François and Jean-Louis left for the North Tower, and Philippe and I looked for a place to hide until dark. We found a pile of electrical equipment under canvas on the floor below and crept in there when no one was around.

It was a *mauvais 2.5 heures*, I can tell you. Hunched under canvas, motionless, roasting, with leg cramps, we could hardly breathe. . . . When it had been quiet for quite a while, we peeked out. It was 7 P.M., and the sun was just beginning to set. We crawled out, crept up the stairs to the roof, and looked out across the chasm to the other tower. There were Jean-Louis and Jean-François, waving. Whoopie.

When it was almost dark, Philippe gave the signal to shoot, and the arrow soared over the gorge and landed nearby. We pulled it over: fishline, fishline, parachute cord, and nylon rope. We were connected, 140 feet across. We had already anchored our side of the cable on the vertical I-beam we had scoped out, and attached the guy lines one-third and two-thirds along its length. Now we knotted its other end to the nylon rope for Jean-Louis and Jean-François to pull across to the North Tower.

We tried to pay it out slowly and keep things under control, but after about seven feet, we couldn't really hold it. It went whooshing out into the void in a giant U. On the other side, Jean-François and Jean-Louis were pulling, but of course it got heavier and heavier the more wire there was. The plan was for them to first use hands, then a pulley, then a triple block-and-tackle unit, then two of them. Once the block-and-tackles were used, it was slow going, a foot at a time, and then reset. Then another foot. Ai, ai, ai. And they were communicating on the intercom that they didn't think they could do it. Too tired. More than 130 feet to go, and it was "just too heavy. We can't move our arms anymore."

So we all took a rest, pumped each other up, and the cable finally made it to the North Tower and was anchored on an I-beam. Philippe and I tightened it with the winch and fastened the guy wires with turnbuckles. It was 6 A.M.—daylight—and everyone was exhausted.

Even though he had not set foot on a high wire for four months, and even though his legs were trembling from fatigue, Philippe felt he was ready. He didn't think, he felt. "Every thought on the wire leads to a fall." His mind was blank.

The big iron wheel began turning at the top of the North Tower: workers were starting to use the elevators. Philippe changed his clothes to black (a *Totentanz?*), put on his slippers, and stepped out over the void. Immediately the wind picked up.

Would *I* do this? Even if I could? Ascension is appealing, but the Fall not so much.

Philippe slowly slid his feet along, and when he was out toward the middle the wire began to sway in the wind. He kept his footing. The wind picked up as he neared the North Tower, but there the cable was more stable. Without hurrying, he walked up to and over the wall. We hadn't discussed a return trip, but there he was, after checking the clamps and guy wires, heading back. Could I watch this again?

Meanwhile, 1,350 feet below, thousands of New Yorkers were doing just that, creating an impressive traffic jam. It turned out the cops had activated the Emergency Jump Plan for suicides. What was that? I wondered. A mop brigade?

Sergeant Daniels and Co. barged up behind me as Philippe was halfway back across. They pushed me aside and yelled out at him, but he stopped ten feet out, spun gracefully around, and set out for a third crossing. It was outrageous: he made seven trips—just out of their reach. He was on the wire for forty-five minutes. Finally Daniels yells at him, "If you don't come off, we'll have a helicopter pick you off." They were dumb enough to do it, too—with the downdraft likely to blow Philippe right off the wire. The yelling seemed to interrupt his concentration, and he stumbled and almost went down. But he recovered, then lay down gently on the wire, his pole across his stomach, maddeningly pretending to take a nap above the void. Maybe he *was* taking a nap. Or listening to the world on this gigantic antenna. Or communing with the Masters of Immobility.

After two minutes or so, he moved his hands to the pole, slid his right foot back till it was under him, and rolled forward until he was hunkered on his right foot, with his left leg still hanging down into the canyon below him. Then he brought himself erect with a powerful thrust of his right leg and began walking again, back to us on the South Tower. He jumped over the wall onto the roof, and handed me his pole. The police burst into applause—then seized him—and me. Jean-François and Jean-Louis had vanished early on. The policeman's lot is not a happy one.

Philippe and I were tried and convicted of trespassing and disturbing the peace, and sentenced to perform for the children in Central Park. We quite fulfilled our sentence, rigging a seven hundred-foot line over Belvedere Lake, anchored to the castle tower, with Philippe walking the incline—the Death Walk: he doesn't know how to swim. Then he went back to France, ending my career as co-conspirator. Now I'll have to look for a *real* job.

Oh, one more thing. I was accepted as a grad student in physics at Cal Tech, starting next week. I'll be working with Feynman on gravitons.

Sorry this is so long, but you always wanted us to write long letters. Maybe you can read it aloud if someone bugs out of a Sabbath lecture.

Say hi to the gang for me, and write if you get a chance.

Love to Sara,

Julius

Nice letter. nice kid. Perhaps it got lost in the mail. There never was an answer.

À La Recherche d'une Femme Perdue

DALETH

On the Danger of Seeking Out Old Lovers

What if they don't remember you? Worse, what if you don't remember them? What if you place them in the wrong time, the wrong school, the wrong job, the wrong town? What if you show such disrespect as to have forgotten the strangling of their mother, or their life-changing auto accident of twenty-five years ago?

Memory, of course, becomes fragile as we get to Julius's age. But some memories *must* be retained—or something is morally suspect. What if you recall that you broke up gently, while the other has thought of you for decades as a despicable fiend? These are things that should not be forgotten. Forget them, and you are a bad person. Remember that you've forgotten them, and you know you are contemptible.

And then, if they ever did, it's likely that they don't love you anymore, that they have taken up with others, have made passionate love, have spawned common children. And where were you? Gone. Done. They went on, didn't need you anymore, and left. Or worse, it was you who walked out—and boy, do you owe them!

And what if they've become ugly, ancient-looking, dumpy? Where is the radiant young face once loved? Somewhere under all that poundage, buried in the bags and wrinkles, suffocated, effaced? What a spectacle! And what if you look equally repellant to them?

Why do we undertake these dangerous expeditions? Gone is gone, done is done, let it go. Let them become the photo in the scrapbook.

We seek them out because they make us remember who we were, and thus, perhaps, who we are. We seek them out because we are humanly curious about how they have gone on. Perhaps they may become new friends.

If the seeker happens to be Julius Marantz, number one on the Central Intelligence Corporation hit list, he may be seeking help.

10.

That Old, Old Love Again

Lydia Lenz, the breath of spring. At least she had been, forty years ago. A Parsifal, Good Friday kind of spring.

Up the steps to Canal, and maybe to Lydia's. Did she still live there? No one gives up a Soho loft. He'd see. The steps up from the station were crowded with beggars, but Julius used the side-stepway, the one too narrow for sitting, set off by spikes. He checked to see if he was being followed. So far so good. At the street exit, he was greeted by a strange, almost artificial sunlight, glinting off the aluminum-foil robes of a vocal quartet:

Bring near Thy great salvation, they sang,
Thou Lamb for sinners slain.

Were they singing to him? The weedy, reedy soprano refused his spare change and sprinted off with her brothers and sister to a site ten steps in front of Julius, where a man was rising slowly upward, screaming in Farsi. And there they sang some more:

Soon may the last glad song arise
Through all the millions of the skies.

Along with four others, Julius scurried under the striped metal awning of Cosmo's Electronic Bizarre to wait out the moment. Two of the four, a couple in their forties, were dressed in fuzzy footed Jammies®, hers pink, his blue. He clutched a teddy, she sucked her blanky as they followed the Korean's rapturous flight. It might have been meant for him, Julius thought.

Lydia Lenz, last of my resources. She came to me so vividly—like the flash of a beacon on a far horizon, blinding, brilliant, unknown—that at first I felt I had to turn away my face. A questionless Catholic, bona fide, the real McCoy.

Our "date" at Saint John the Divine, she and I, thighs pressed together on crowded cushioned pew. I was afraid of polluting her with my Mischlinge *spirit. The coldness of her hand, warmed by my own, entropy increasing. And then the chant—majestic, incontrovertible tones enveloping the text. All other sound henceforth shallow. But there we were, tangled in it, postulated on its plane, beyond the veil of Maya, through the gates. And all was possible before us.*

A car drove by, bristling with antennae, "Central Intelligence Corporation" emblazoned in gay supergraphics over its entire frame, on top an ad, like a sign for pizza, the smiley face with glasses on Julius's bag, with the jingle text "You and me and the CIC." The driver looked at the bearded old guy while talking on his cellular.

You helped me make the change. Conversion of my conversion, air at the anaerobic heights. Our midnight mass that Christmas, with the crèche at the side of the sanctuary, its fir boughs banked around a little stable. Their scent, their resinous scent assaulting my spirit. In the scent of that scent I saw us for the first time, not as simply existing but as created things, factum non genitum, *witnesses to the Word, the divine Logos, who made our souls in His image, made them with intent, made them out of love.*

"Spare change, Mister? For a good Christian?"

Julius passed by unawares, deep in his Lydia reverie.

"Fuck you!" the man called after him, "in Jesus' name."

Smell of fir cut across everything else in the heart of my heart, so far from home and Judaism. In shul I'd felt some spiritual intensity, latent, remnant—but so mixed with stultifying convention and complacency. While here, with you . . .

I sensed a promise that if I came to Christ, really came, He would not demand that I renounce the physical world. It was His world, of His making, for me to take, to study, a world in which to understand complexity, His complexity, the externals of things in which He is hidden, to seek for the Reality behind them. That smell, that pine-tree smell: atoms of God against my nose.

A five-year-old offered the nice old man a spoiled tomato. He didn't notice.

Shepherds. I'd never even seen a real shepherd. What were they to me? But the fir scent brought me back beyond New York, beyond cities and so-called civilization. Back to old European forests, ancestors, Jewish ancestors living roughly, hand to mouth and hand to hand. And with your hand in mine, and that incense around us, those shepherds with their rough hands came alive, and with them the meaning and wonder of the Incarnation. Et homo factus est! *And I too became a man, a connected man, bar mitzvah in Christ, in the wonder of that moment. With you. In the giant, obscure cosmos. Among the molecules of fir.*

Julius threaded his way among a village of street-people huts camped Tuesdays, Thursdays, and Saturdays on the south side of the street. Tonight they would move, or be buried in the Monday, Wednesday, Friday shift of garbage from north to south. Rat-like humans with long sticks were harvesting produce through the razor wire surrounding a pocket park.

• • •

Some Catholic I was before YOU! *More of a pantheist, I would say, hungering for a center—I-Am-Who-Am deflated to I-Am-What-Is. Mere physics. Hope I had. But faith? Before you, just pious, adolescent self-deception, just untrammeled self, hunting across the categories. Before you, before then, even love, even love was a fiction, my "insight" into the oneness of all things; a physicist's notion of love, some kind of shining gravitational flow, a sublimation from necessity, a cheap evasion of loneliness. Before you, and the fir, and the living God.*

Physicists, being things, love things and the sequencing of things. You changed all that.

Newsstand headline: 300 RAPTURED IN INDIA. GOVERNMENT APPLAUDS FAITHFUL. It focused his vision and snatched him from reverie, and a good thing, too, for he was now surrounded by a small chorus of prisoner angels, eponymously striped and winged, and would have collided with the circle had he not looked up and around.

At first they sang slowly:

I want a sober mind
An all-sustaining eye,

And then fast and fugueing:

I'd soar away above the sky
I'd fly, fly, fly
To see my God above.

"You can't leave. We're not finished," whispered a stunningly threatening alto. And Julius stopped to listen to the rest. Performances, performances, performances, he thought; the world has become one big, self-sustaining show.

Before the fugueing tune could repeat, a counterdemonstration began. Ten "radical Muslim housewives" in boots and burkas arrived, holding printed signs—IT'S ONLY HINDUS!—THE END OF THE WORLD IS NOT AT HAND!—and distracted the chorus, who broke sacred cadence to counterattack. Julius was able to push through the crowd, ahead toward Mercer. Five more blocks to (hopefully) Lydia's.

CRASH!

Not one foot in front of him, a flowerpot smashed to the ground. No flower. A pot filled with incinerator ashes. Julius looked up. "Sorry," a woman above said.

He walked quickly past an empty lot. Among the trash and rusting vehicles, several children had strung a rope over the crane pulley of a wrecked tow truck. A child was being lifted into the air by a rope around his waist as the other sang.

All around the tearful Earth
The Devil chased the Christian

Till Jesus reached out all in mirth—

Up goes the Christian!

The tune cross-faded with "The Hallelujah Chorus" coming east on Canal Street, and the children broke up their game and went running toward the All Popes' Day parade. A huge float rolled slowly through the teeming streets as dogs and humans swarmed around it. Julius was swept along by the mob. It was good to feel relatively safe.

On the float, surrounded by orchestra and blue-robed choir, a huge, baked, crucified Christ was nailed to a cross painted with corporate logos. A Pope-costumed figure tore off pieces of Christ's body and tossed the bread to the surging, hungry crowd. Ecclesiastical Police attempted, violently, to keep order. A second Pope figure worked an electronic organ grinder, and led the crowd in a chant of "Take! Eat! Yum yum yum!" At the rear of the float, male and female bikini angels threw Celestial Condoms™ to the crowd.

Julius was almost crushed as he stooped to pick up a piece of fallen bread. Someone grabbed it out of his hand and stuffed it into his own mouth. Julius smiled politely, meekly apologized, and managed to work his way beyond the edge of the crowd to detour down Greene Street, avoiding the parade. Signs in storefront after storefront pierced his heart with guilt. *He* was responsible, none but he.

LOVE HAS CONQUERED EVIL. DIAL

1-800-MESSIAH.

and

BUY NOW, PERHAPS PAY NEVER!

and

BRING OUT BEHEMOTH!

Oi! Best to blinker. Ears closed, eyes down, avoid human contact.

He took a right on Broadway at the 300 block, a neighborhood of cast-iron commercial buildings he remembered from the old days. But, unlike in the old days, they had been repainted alternating pink and blue. Over each entrance, not only a street number but a name writ large, with accompanying graphic: Canaan Towers Apartlets; Jordan Banks Apartlets; Narrow Gate Apartments; Beulah Land Coops. 371; the Needle's Eye Garden Apartlets and its logo, the Great Seal Eye. Needle and camel must have been elsewhere.

In the lobby, Julius found two doormen with movie-star faces and chocolate-smeared mouths. In small print, on the right sides of their necks, the Biotech Corp. logo. Julius smiled politely.

"Mornin', fellas."

The doormen eyed him with suspicion.

"Wuh-doo-yuh-wahn, Grahn-da-dee?"

Julius pulled two small Natural Flakes™ bags from his pack and held them up before the Cerberi. When the doormen moved to grab them, Julius pulled them back.

"Not so fast . . . not so fast." He overenunciated his good-natured words. Then, in a sweetly seductive singsong, "Let me in."

"Ooh-kayee, Grahn-da-dee. Gim mee dee flake-ess."

Julius handed over the flakes and in one quick move ran up the stairs. Out of breath, pale and sweating at the first floor, he tried the elevator—which didn't work—and continued up, climbing ever more slowly, to the sixth floor.

Exhausted, with incipient anginal pain, Julius pounded on the tin door, denting it inadvertently. A large dog began to bark behind it.

A voice rang out from inside. It was the old voice, the voice that had so buoyed him, the voice of Lydia Lenz.

"Who the hell is it?"

"It's Julius, Lydia."

Nothing.

"Julius Marantz. Lydia, please open the door."

"Julius?"

"I'm being followed, Lydia. Could you please open the door?"

Behind the door, silence. Then three bolts unbolted, and the door opened to the limit of the three-inch chain. Thirty-six years sidled through the crack. That, and the smell of fried fish.

Old, she thought. He looks so old.

Old, he thought. She looks so old.

Do I look that old? he wondered.

Do I look that old?

For sixty, she was attractive, and might have been forty-five. A weary forty-five. But as the door opened, Julius could concentrate only on the pit bull attacking him with licking. Lydia's first concern was to calm him.

"Alabama, down. Down. Good boy. Good boy."

Her next concern was to calm Julius, who, as soon as she was reachable, threw himself upon her in gratitude. She fended him off with the Abby statuette she had brought to the door for protection. He positive, she negative: Julius pulled back, Scottie-like, from the asymmetry, and they stared at each other and remembered. Then Julius collapsed on the floor in anginal pain.

"Oh no," she said. "Are you having one of your—your—panic attacks?"

"No, no. It's my heart. My pills. In pocket. In my pocket. Under my tongue."

Lydia got down on the floor, searched his pants pockets, found and administered the nitro. As he sat with head down and eyes closed, attending to the arterioles, she took his hand.

"Are you OK?"

That voice, the old honey voice, languid, melodious, seductive.

"Yeah, yeah. I'm OK."

"Julius, what the hell is going on with you? I haven't seen you since—what?—1967, and you come crashing in here like Rambo, or some drug-crazed Deadhead. Where on Earth did you find this shirt? And take off that phony beard."

"They're after me."

"Who?"

"The CIC, the FBI, the DOD, the EPA, the DOE, the COG, the . . ."

Lydia got up to get him a drink, her gray hair windblown even in no wind.

"Hyperbole, Julius. Paranoia. Are you still smoking pot?"

In the kitchenette, she rinsed a glass with grayish-yellow tap water, removed a jug of clean water from a locked cabinet, and filled a glass. The strains from one of the choruses rose up from outside:

Oh, who will come and go with me,
We'll shout and sing Hosanna.

Carefully taking a sip from the overfilled glass, she wound her way back and offered Julius the water, her delicate hands more freckled, her face still winning, yet with a tiredness beneath her eyes. Julius knew her, and he didn't.

After a long drink and a short sigh, he struggled up to sit on an antique futon sofa.

"Thanks" was all he could say.

For the next minute, they simply breathed together, he in his disguise, she in her long-sleeved Notre Dame t-shirt with Cimabue madonna on the back.

"You're still a beautiful woman," he dared.

"It has ceased to be with me after the manner of women," she noted.

Julius nodded. He looked around the tiny room (a subdivision of her often-subdivided loft). which was crammed with '60s and '70s antiques. There were several framed Lydia Lenz posters on the walls, and a photo of her being awarded her Abby. A blue-and-white "Catholic Workers" banner was draped over the couch. A large screen TV dominated the apartlet.

"My life has become quite implausible, Lydia."

"What a surprise," she said.

He told her about his visit to the Executive Office Building, about the meeting with GEKO, about Babson's money and his challenge. Her eyes shone. He worked back to his accident, the MRI, and the genesis of the Doodad idea—about which more anon. He had to start from scratch on electromagnetism, about how moving electrons give rise to magnetic fields, how, in principle, such fields are unlimited in force, but that wire coils tend to explode when the forces surpass their tensile strength. At the Middlebury Mag Lab, he could create a field of about two million gauss before his instruments would self-destruct.

"Self-destruction seems to be a theme here," she observed.

Good old Lydia. But she did seem fascinated.

"How strong are my refrigerator magnets?" she asked. "Just to get a sense."

"About two hundred gauss. The largest permanent magnet, maybe three thousand gauss."

"And you went to two million? How did you manage that?"

"Little by little, explosion by explosion. Electrical resistance goes down with temperature, so I needed cold, cold, cold. Liquid helium, then solid helium. Very expensive, but very cold—right down near absolute zero. At those temperatures, things usually go superconductive. But that was the rub: superconductivity is destroyed by an intense magnetic field."

"Bummer," she remarked. The old language of their once time kicked his heart into his throat. He swallowed.

"The key to the Doodad was discovering that superconductivity reestablishes in even stronger fields. I was able to push the flux higher than had ever been done."

"No explosions?"

"Yes explosions. And enormous heat. But all contained in a huge zirconium steel vessel." He threw his arms out to show her how immense. "I suspended the coils on zirconium oxide, fifty layers of copper-niobium wire, the strongest conductor ever. And to minimize the chance of meltdown, I only went for pulsed fields, fifty milliseconds at most."

Most of the nouns were exotic to her. But she watched, fascinated, as the old Julius came into focus, like a slowly developing print. She felt she'd best apply the fixative.

"So let me see if I get it." She stood up with what seemed some difficulty and began to pace. "You made this monster magnetic field, and by pointing it first at mice, then hamsters, cats, dogs, and now humans, you were able to polarize all the water molecules in Joe Shmoe, line them up so that Mr. Shmoe becomes an organic magnet . . ."

". . . polarized in opposition to the earth, south to south, north to north . . ."

". . . and then, like those little Scotty dogs that push each other away . . ."

". . . the earth's field pushes Joe Shmoe off the face of the planet . . ."

". . . and GEKO, you say, finds this . . . constructive?"

"Beneficent."

She nodded, and took it all in stride. "And you don't find it beneficent."

"Look around you," Julius said.

"Could be worse," she observed.

"It can't go on like this."

"Oh no? Walter Benjamin said that 'for the suffering of individuals as of communities, there is only one limit beyond which things cannot go: annihilation.'"

Only silence could be the answer. And then. . .

"Been studying up on Benjamin, have you?"

"Isn't this the time for it?"

"Not for me. I intend to do something more practical."

"And what is that?"

"Spill the beans, that's what. I'm going to spill the beans. *We're* going to spill the beans—to let the world know what's actually going on with these so-called raptures. I came because I need you to make a film about this—film me and my story, film my lab and my demonstration experiments, so if they do get me, you can get this information out."

"So then they can get *me?*" she asked.

Julius hadn't thought that far.

"Have you told GEKO your plans?"

"I sent a letter. On Wednesday."

"What sort of letter?'

"A letter of intent. They must have gotten it."

"How do you know?"

"There was a wanted sequence for me at a movie today."

"In a public theater?"

"Yes."

She looked at his eyes then and saw. . . . "Let's go for a walk," she said.

"I can't go out in the street, Lydia. They've got the CIC, the KGB, Scotland Yard . . ."

"I know, I know. You told me. But let's go for a walk. We'll disguise you. It's safer to talk outside. Besides, we should get a paper."

"Disguise me? I'm already disguised."

"Here—wait . . ."

Lydia shuffled around in her closet and came up with a long down coat, a huge wide-brimmed hat with a big bow, and a knitted ski mask.

"A down coat in June?" He laughed. "Oh, that'll get me through!"

"You're probably right."

"You're hopeless."

"'It's for those without hope that hope is given.'"

A Benjamin response to an old Julius accusation.

She returned to rummage again in her closet. As she reentered the room with a long raincoat, a wide-brimmed Chinese cotton sun hat, and a long silk scarf, the TV clicked on, unrequested, to the end of a Christian game show with its applause and laughter, hooting and shouting. Julius gave a huge groan.

"Just ignore it," she said. "It's hopeless to try to stop it. Believe me." And she began a search for fashionable accoutrements.

"Before we close, we have a few personal messages for some special brothers and sisters. Maria, we hope to join you soon in the promised land. Mom and Dad. . . . Julius, Grandma—says—hello. . . . Emily . . ."

Julius turned to the TV, stunned.

"Oh God, oh God. You know what that means, Lydia? 'Grandma says hello'? They're gonna rapture me."

His movements were now quite shaky. He took the costume from Lydia and put it on as quickly as he could. She took two pills while he was dressing.

"Come on. We've got to get out of here."

The game show dissolved to an ad for the Central Intelligence Corporation. Alabama began whining and turning in circles.

"Quiet! Stay!" Lydia ordered, and he did. As Julius reached the door, the phone began to ring. Lydia made a move to answer it, but he grabbed her arm.

"No! Let it ring."

While the phone insisted, Lydia squeezed a large white glob from a wall dispenser at the door and applied sunscreen to his face. Those hands, the cool hands he loved. As she applied the Creem™ to her own face and hands, Julius—even in the midst of his agitation—looked at her with longing. Thoughts he had—like the fleeting, irrelevant thoughts of a condemned man being strapped onto the table. Lydia stood a moment with her eyes closed, her slender fingers rubbing white into her glowing cheeks. Old love twinged through his panic, a shiver through fevered flesh.

"Hurry up," he said.

HE

Why Would Anyone Want to Rapture Julius Marantz?

Middlebury College

Department of Physics

Middlebury VT 05753-0661-467

6 June 2003

Dear Fr. Thornbottom,

Two years ago, you and I sat together at Carolyn Worthington's and spoke of many things. I was particularly moved by your love of Dostoevsky's Christ, the Godman who could answer the Grand Inquisitor with a kiss. That tale, you said, played a decisive role in your life, persuading you to enter the church to serve Him.

I have thought many times since then about our talk, and have twice reread that immense work which so inspired you. For that, I must thank you. But now I share with you the path it has sent me on, a trajectory which lands me in a place at this point so different from your own. In Dostoyevsky, it is the Lord's silence which triumphs. I, however, can no longer be silent. While I cannot be Christ, or even serve Him as you do, I *can* be a Julius-Alyosha, and embrace the foolishness of the cross, if not its wisdom. And so I write.

I write in a world of madness, the bewildering and outrageous world you and I and GEKO have played a key part in creating. It is a devil's vaudeville out there, a world of illusion, a huge miasma in which it is impossible to avoid wrong-doing and sin. Our hearts no longer beat for one another but long only for release, and unknowingly for destruction. Everything is gussied up as games, children's games with songs and hymns and dances—none of which are as innocent as they appear, for they disguise a planet-wide renunciation of love and of God.

The seat of the disease is arrogance, and GEKO is both its major symptom and its chief victim. Like the Grand Inquisition of sixteenth-century Seville, GEKO has "corrected" Christ, embraced the temptations He rejected:

—Earth Friends' *miracle* of earthly "bread" and air and water restored, its eaters and breathers and drinkers reduced to manageable numbers. . .

—the Council of Churches' valorization of *mystery,* a mystery which exists only for the masses who don't understand the magnetics of the current rapture. . .

—the Administration's *authority* in choosing the sacrificial elect from among the politically problematic people of the ever-expanding Axis of the Unwilling.

Miracle, mystery, and authority, the great Trinity of the Grand Inquisitor and his regime. Does this not raise a warning flag for you? "We are not with thee but with *the other,*" the Grand Inquisitor admitted; "that is our secret." Is that GEKO's secret, too? In this time of psychological imbalance, when all our old landmarks are gone, with no new ones in sight, will GEKO's improvements on the work of God add up to the coming of the Antichrist?

Perhaps I'm being harsh. Perhaps I am simply not accepting what is a practical, rational truth: that as GEKO says, it is *good* for people to turn again to the church; it is *good* for populations to be reduced and for America's enemies to dwindle. But—don't you see?—that rational truth is not the truth of Christ, but of Pilate. The truth of Ivan, not of Alyosha.

GEKO thinks people will reject goodness unless and until it is accompanied by the end of the world. But that is because GEKO—not you, perhaps, but GEKO—*does not believe in God.* And therefore, it does not believe in man. It loves humanity tolerantly but autocratically, contemptuously. What is the price of GEKO's truth? With what frenzy and chaos and ultimate violence is it to be purchased?

I address this letter to you, Father, and not to the others because if it were mathematically proven that truth is not in Christ, you and I would still adhere to Him rather than to truth. But we both know Truth when we confront it. Why, then, are we dealing in the business of the Lie? You and I believe in God, not in the Doodad, and because of that, we cannot accept a world the Doodad brings. It is now our role, the role of the fallen, to rebel from Hell and rise to God again—not by megahertz but by megaheart—for humankind and for Truth.

An old rabbi once warned me—his young intellectual and physicist-to-be—that the opposite of love is not hate but rather the ruminations of the brain. While the heart loves, it is the brain that judges and blames. How true: we do not worship the Sacred Brain of Jesus. We must not blame the members of GEKO, but we must undo their deeds—and forgive them. I, for one, long to forgive everyone, to beg forgiveness for all of us, for all and everything.

I will be holding a press conference on these matters on 28 June, and I invite you to join me, to alert GEKO, and to invite its members' participation or comments.

With faith in the kiss of Jesus,

Julius-Alyosha Marantz

Not a bad letter. It was enough to get him condemned.

Albert Einstein once said, "If A equals success, then the formula is A = X + Y +Z, where X is work, Y is play, and Z is keep your mouth shut."

Neither was Julius very good at it.

11.

For in Thy Dark Streets Shineth

The gravity-assisted stairs were easy down, as Julius and Lydia descended to the lobby. The doormen, halfway through a carton of Heavenly Hunks™, flashed Lydia a three-fingered signal and didn't bat an eye at her strange-looking companion.

"What is that?" Julius asked.

"What?"

"That sign they gave you. The three fingers. We don't have that in Vermont."

He pushed open the great door and beckoned Lydia to precede him down the iron steps to the street.

"It's the 'E-sign.' I'm not sure what it means. Earthling or Everyman or Elect or Ecowarrior; who knows? It's a wild card—it can mean anything."

"Erebus, the place of darkness? The Evil One?"

"Could be."

The streets were yet more crowded as people fled midday

asphyxiation in their apartlets. The pink and blue buildings flaunted their floral designs, their fluted columns, their arches and decorative keystones framing wide windows filled with posters to block the unblocked sun.

"HE SHALL CHANGE OUR VILE BODY," the graffiti advised, "THAT IT MAY BE FASHIONED LIKE UNTO HIS GLORIOUS BODY" (PHILIPPIANS 3:21).

Lydia pointed her chin south, down West Broadway, to the blue sky once commandeered by the World Trade Center.

"You like the view?" she asked.

"The falcon cannot hear the falconer," Julius said.

"There's a certain freedom in that, wouldn't you say? For both?"

He remembered their old arguments. Whatever he said, she said the opposite. Old. The arguments were old, and so were they. His chest began to ache, and the ache was not anginal.

"That's my church there, across the street, Saint Joseph's. We can go in, if you like, if you're afraid to be out."

"No. We'd best talk out of doors. Let's just keep moving."

They turned the corner onto Grand. Mansard roofs gazed down; cornices and dormers stared.

CHURCH OF THE QUIVERING BRETHREN, said 72 Grand. CHURCH OF WHAT'S HAPPENING RIGHT NOW, announced its neighbor. The

Whore Megastore at 80–88 featured a banner with three men in bulging briefs. WHEN THE MESSIAH COMES HE'LL BE WEARING CLEAN UNDERWEAR. CALVIN KLEIN, it announced.

A CIC car passed up Green Street in front of them, followed by the six-piece Fart of God Marching Orchestra (so said the bass drum), the eponymous fart being rhythmically emitted by what looked like a full-blooded psychopath, wrapped in chains, staggering under the weight of a contrabassoon, carried on his back like a cross. They played a quite recognizable version of the Ninth Symphony march, which segued neatly into their "Ode to Joy." The back-balanced contra forced its player to bend grotesquely to reach the reed. A flag on his endpin said, "ZEITGEIST MUSIC PRESENTS."

"More parades than usual," Lydia remarked.

"Why is that?"

"It's God Blesses America Day Five, I think."

"Ah. I've lost track."

And then, an amazing metamorphosis: A flip of the contra off the back, a different skin cover for the drum, a general change of hats, a 90-degree turn, and the Fart of God Marching Orchestra was transmogrified into Fling Badhair and the Unforeseens, launching into their signature song:

I wanna fly to the sky with you, baby,
Get high as a pie with you, baby,
Try unh to die,

Put lye in your eye,
Cyanide pie,
Spy when you cry and you do, baby,
Shout out good-bye, good-bye, good-bye,
Good-bye, good-bye, good-bye, good-bye . . .

Eastward Fling marched, to take its message to Little Italy, perhaps, and behind them, their anatine mascots, all in a row. "Aw, look at the ducks," said a fat woman. "Ducks is cute."

WAW

Beethoven and the Voice of God

And the eternal voice does, indeed, speak today, just as it did in times immemorial. But as then, now too, one requires preparation to be able to hear it.

—MARTIN BUBER, *THE TEN RUNGS OF HASIDIC LORE*

The Fart of God Marching Orchestra was not just another collection of church-band escapees. How many amateur musicians own a $15,000 Heckel contrabassoon? Or a Kruspe horn, or a genuine York tuba? No, FOGMO was made up of born-again members of the Metropolitan Opera Orchestra who, exhausted from more than four hundred consecutive performances of *Parsifal,* needed to get out into the streets for some fresh air. Toxic as it was, it was less damaging than never-ending Wagner.

These guys could play. Theirs were the embouchures of the archangel Gabriel, at least, if not of YHWH Himself. They had all played the Ninth Symphony many times (back in the old days), and knew it inside out. Their understanding was in terms simultaneously musical, theological, and philosophical; it was that of all good musicians. And like all good musicians, they referred to the opening of the last movement's *alla Marcia* as "the fart of God." Six inexplicable bursts of the contrabassoon, a sound never before featured in human music, became the rhythmic spine for a syncopated tenor solo about suns flying through the vast and glorious abysses of space, and mortals assumed therein.

Why this soundscape? many had wondered, and have been wondering since 1825. To FOGMO, the answer was obvious:

Beethoven, the sufferer, the particular victim of stomach disease, devoted his great late-period genius to exploring spiritual triumph over psychic and somatic pain. Not a churchy man, he was nevertheless profoundly religious, as witnessed not only by the Ninth Symphony but by the great *Missa Solemnis*. He believed in the divine afflatus—and from both ends, as who in his condition would not?

Beethoven was a "romantic," but of a quite different sort from those who followed him. He was "iconoclasm transformed into a moral force" (Mellers), and part of that iconoclasm was to be a conscious ruffian among "the princely rabble." His farts—God's Farts within him—were consciously employed. Hearing them in the Ninth Symphony requires only the suspension of disbelief that "the great Beethoven" of *classical* music would never refer to such a low animal function. Of course he would. That's why he was Beethoven.

The metamorphosis of FOGMO to Fling Badhair and the Unforeseens was no accident either. In an 1890 letter to his publishers, Breitkopf and Härtel, the Master signed off thusly: "I wish you all that is good and beautiful, inasmuch as our wild century permits." Fling Badhair was that wild century—only three years in. What would it be like in ten? That was the Unforeseen. But their signature song said it all.

These guys could really wail.

12.

Zekiel Saw the Wheel

FIGHT ROAD RAGE WITH HONDA LITHIUM, said a sign. HOLOCAUST IS OURS FOREVER, said another.

"We might be safer in the crowd," Julius said. He took Lydia's arm and pulled her along as a second flowerpot crashed down behind them, shattering its bird of paradise and spotting Julius's raincoat with mud and loam. The gargoyles smiled from between their sixth-floor spandrels. The couple scurried on ahead as best they could.

Lydia was feeling weak. She leaned on his arm and tugged him away from the crowd.

"I thought you liked these Catholic Worker kind of folks," he teased.

"What gets me about *these* people," Lydia said, "is that they have no real relation to Christianity."

"Like me?" Julius bristled, apprehensive at the return of old battles. But Lydia, too, did not want to fight. It was why they had split up, or rather, had not truly come together. She needed him now, his arm.

Julius remembered her depth compared to his, her commitment and his dalliance, the fierce laser of her eyes and the watery blue of his own.

She pushed on. "If Jesus was mocked and spat upon, then *Christianity* is what's mocked and spat upon. No way out. A spat-upon Jesus means spat-upon churches, spat-upon theology, spat-upon fight against evil. Not the comfort of bishops, right? Or academics. Not the feet-up power of some kind of Big Fella. Serving Jesus means being ready to be spat upon. Spitters are superficial; the spat-upon are profound. Being spat upon—that's our life and our healing. No more, no less."

Julius walked with her in silence back down Grand.

YOU CAN'T TAKE IT WITH YOU—

GIVE BLOOD TODAY.

CACHEXIA CRUNCH™ BY

GENERAL FOODS. YUM!

When had Julius Marantz, full professor of physics and Nobel nominee, been mocked or spat upon? Was he a good Christian, a good Catholic, or a good Jew? They continued in silence as an angel passed slowly over. From out of the flustered hush between them:

CRASH! Bounce, bounce.

A four-slice toaster fell out of the sky, three feet in front of them. *That* brought her back.

And WHONGO! Bada, bada, bada, a waffle iron disgorged its plates against the sidewalk behind them, its plug-in cord unplugging and whipping the ground like an unhinged serpent. They stopped dead in their tracks. From a fifth-floor balustrade, a ten-year-old waved.

Julius limping, Lydia trying to keep up. From behind them, the quiet sound of roaring, getting louder. Julius looked back apprehensively. It was not the CIC or the DOD or the NSA but a fleet of motorcycles, slowly approaching, wending its way almost—but not quite—politely through the crowd in the street.

"THE ZEKIEL WHEELERS," it said on their backs, Their emblem a Harley heading upward into a cross-filled cloud.

"'Scuse me, man, 'scuse me, lady," said a gargantuan rider, easy on his hog, riding on the sidewalk. Julius pulled Lydia back against the wall.

Frightened, exhausted, out of breath, but suspecting that even Central Intelligence would avoid this bunch, the two of them climbed up to rest high on a stoop in a doorway under a protecting cornice. The bikers seemed friendly enough, if fierce-looking—large, long-haired men in black leather. The women were more diverse—made-up and natural, long-haired and short, bosomy and thin as rails.

Directly across the street, beyond the mustering of bikes, a striking blond, her hair rising heavenward in pentecostal do, bullhorned the group to order. Those poor fans wishing to follow the Fart of God or Fling Badhair to Little Italy had to inch through the bikes and around them.

The crowd sang together, in raucous harmony, the "Our Lady Anthem," a hymn to the immaculate Virgin, imploring her

To be our salvation from death, hell and sin,
Which our transgression involvèd us in.

A man took up the bullhorn.

"Bon-*do*, Bon-*do*," the crowd chanted.

"Who is that?" Julius asked a hefty biker, come up the stoop to get a better view.

"That's Bondo Brad," Magoo said, "our president. A heavy dude. Great man. You'll see."

Brad was not a man of the cloth but a man of the skin, black leather, collared in white, and shawled in the Zekiel Wheelers' flag, ruby red, with a white central circle framing the hog, the clouds, and the cross. Huge but gaunt, cheeks red—in skin most pale, voice intense, and quick of speech.

"Brothers and sisters in Christ, sons and daughters of Ezekiel, papas and mamas of celestial chariots," he intoned through the bullhorn, "I want to talk to you about—hogs!"

Wild cheering from the congregation.

"Hold thy peace and perpend. The subject of my talk, dear

brother blockheads, refers not to your glorious machines but to you, especially those male persons whose average weight is—what?—two hundred fifty pounds? Three hundred? How, *how* are you ever gonna get to heaven when the rapture comes? Three hundred pounds of meat flying through the air?"

Cheers. "Meat, meat, meat!"

Julius and Lydia surveyed the scene. It made him think of some gross beer hall, but one with Schubert in it, writing lieder on the tablecloth, or Picasso in a steak house, modeling animals from bread. What beasts these men were. And their painted molls. Pagans to his and Lydia's Christian.

Lydia, on the other hand, squinted, framed them in her mind, and saw them as characters in a fairy tale—diabolic mutations, perhaps, but a means of revealing beauty.

An AWACSoCopt passed by, high over the canyon of the street.

"Instead of opening the beer bottle or the fridge," Bondo bull-horned, "I want you to open the connection between you and God. Let us examine text."

Out of forty saddlebags came forty Bibles for sixty pairs of eyes.

"In Exodus 16, God turns his people's manna into maggots to keep them from hoarding. Hoarding, eating every scrap, shows lack of trust that the Lord will provide. Maggots for them that hoards and gorges. Maggots for you!

"Most churches in this blubbery land use food to lure worshippers—suppers and soup kitchens; sanctimonious feasts of pizza, franks, and fries; ice-cream socials. You Christians are fatter than most because you've forgotten that gluttony is a sin. You say, 'Bring hither the fatted calf.' Right? What *do* you say?"

Only a distant siren was heard. Julius's ears pricked up.

"I can't hear you. Do you say, 'Help, Lord—The Devil wants me fat'? Do you say, 'More of Jesus, less of me'? No, you hogs would rather worship Little Debbie and her Devil Dogs." Bondo intoned:

> Which way I fly is hell; myself am hell;
> And in the lowest deep a lower deep . . .

"My God," Julius thought, "it's . . ." Bondo Brad a Miltonist! You can't tell a book by its cover.

"You! You, up, up, up." Bondo Ben pointed across the street to Julius, fixed him with glittering eye. "I mean you, the lady with the raincoat and Chinese hat. You with that lovely blue silk scarf. Come down here and stand by me."

Faraday, Maxwell, Bohr, Einstein—men of integrity and wholeness of character, Julius thought. Generous, benign. Not like these. These are not my people.

"Go on," Magoo nudged. "He won't eat you. Not in front of his wife."

Should he do it? Why was he undecided? With Lydia's push, Julius limped down the steps, pardoned his way across the street, and stepped up onto the stoop, the show of some unimagined telling, Public Exhibit Number 1—in drag.

"What's your name, ma'am?"

"Uh, Julia," he answered.

"Julia, I have a question. Would you prefer a thin, handsome man like me or one of those repulsive behemoths out there?"

Julia was too shy to say. She pointed instead. Boos and hisses from the crowd. Bondo thanked his guest, clapped her hard on the back, and sent her back to her friend on the stoop across the street. A street bum snapped their portrait with a digital SLR.

"Hey, mister, don't . . ." Julius cried, but he was gone.

"You see?" Bondo cried, "The natural state of man is slender. Julia loved slender. All women love slender."

"'Ceptin ours!" a hog hippo yelled, to widespread mollulation.

"But you," Bondo continued, imperturbable, "*you* decided to pray to Little Debbie—and look where she's got you. You know what you need? Big-time exercise. You need to drop your carcasses down on your knees fifty times a day to pray—and lug 'em back up again. You want sweets? God is sweeter than a Baby Ruth, with bigger nuts. You, my friends, will have to die to your will. Look at me. Do I look dead from dying? Don't I look happy?"

To demonstrate, he broke into a song—with gestures:

The bells of hell go ding-a-ling-a-ling
For you, and not for me.

Oh Death, where is thy sting-a-ling-a-ling

O grave, thy victory?

"Deliver us from Little Debbie. Amen."

And he turned the bullhorn back to the do, stalked down the steps, and sat glumly on his bike.

The crowd cheered and broke out the beer and the Ding Dongs. It was adequately weird. There were gunshots in the distance. After all the flashbulbs, Julius and Lydia felt the urgent need to move on.

"Not so fast, you."

A voice from inside a little hut hitched behind a green Harley at the curb. Julius wanted to keep going, but Lydia pulled him back. JAKOB BEN-AUSCHWITZ, it said on the rear. And under that, HE SUKKOTH.

"Lydia, no. Let's keep moving."

She pulled him up the two steps into the hut, intrepid, even in extremis.

Inside he sat, Jakob Ben-Auschwitz, hissing at them as they pushed on through the flap, then beckoning them in, a huge old spider, big as a barn, white of tooth, red-hairy of head, face, and hand, and wrapped in a blue-and-white tallis like the one stored in the back of Julius's closet. Sing yikes at the red, white, and blue.

"*Shalom aleichem,* ladies," he croaked, and *"Aleichem shalom,"* Julius mumbled back.

"The Lord is our butcher, He shall not haunt," said the spider, and from under his tallis he thrust out his forearm. It said, "73860."

"It's God keeps me from doing it," he said. "If it was up to me, I'd be robbing your handbags right now. There's very little good left."

"Where'd you get the tattoo?" Lydia asked, interviewing. "Which camp?"

"Auschwitz?" Julius asked. The spider nodded.

"Nice ink, no?" he said.

They didn't know what to reply.

"Look," the spider growled, "if God calls it, God pays. Only paranoid schizophrenics think there's some conspiracy to do them harm. Or good. Either one. Want some hemp? Wacky-baccy for the ladies?"

He offered up a smoldering bong, the glass elaborately engraved with Hebrew letters.

"No, thank you," they said, though they both could have used some.

"I thought you might be Jewish. Two Jewish ladies. So I want to show you something."

"What's that?" Lydia asked.

"Something I got during the war."

Jakob Ben-Auschwitz unbuttoned his fly and took out a small, unthreatening penis.

"See this?"

Julius tried to bolt, but Lydia stopped him, still the documentarian, if now without her camera. Together they focused clinically on what Jakob was pointing to—the small blue-black tattoo, a star of David, limp along the penile side, like a melting Dali clock.

"Shut the tent flap,"

Lydia reached over and flipped the canvas closed.

"Watch this," the spider said. "Follow the star of redemption."

Jakob Ben-Auschwitz closed his eyes, and Julius and Lydia fixed their anxious gaze on the Mogen David. God knows what was going on behind Jakob's weighty lids. It could have been women or freshly dead corpses; it could have been elegant equations or gelatin desserts. But slowly the organ began to expand along its axis. What had been two inches grew into nine; inked lines emerged from folds, collapsing centrally, elongating, stretching, extending along the growing shaft; a star become thrust only, length, the upright of . . . a cross, a blue-black cross, a crucifix whose transom was a pulsing vessel, also blue-black, beating like a sacred heart, the brachial arteries of ghostly arms.

The Sukkoth hut began to shake, then tilt, then rise underfoot like Einstein's elevator. Julius made a leap through the canvas and pulled Lydia out with him. Sprawled on the sidewalk, surrounded by

CNNNN camcorders, they watched the hut ascend, pulling the Harley along behind it. From inside they could hear Jakob Ben-Auschwitz singing *Yitgadal v'yitkadash* as he rose into the sky, his Mogen David growing ever more the cross. Around the scene, the bikers cheered and danced and whooped and whistled and sang.

'Tis finished! all is finished,
His fight with death and sin:
Fling open wide the golden gates,
And let the victor in.
U.S.A., NUMBER ONE! U.S.A., NUMBER ONE!

As hut and hog drifted upward and northward, they turned their bikes around, vroom-vroom, and roared away to follow and serenade them as best they could. For the space of a minute, it was noisier than usual in the earth and the heavens.

Julius and Lydia were left shaking, leaning against the corner of West Broadway and Grand, half a block from Lydia's church. Perhaps Saint Joseph could protect them for a while.

A small, bedraggled child with two black roses cried after them, *"Flores, chicas? Flores para los muertos?"*

13.

The Fall of a Sparrow

Lydia led her old new friend through the Grand Street fence into a side yard, overgrown, along a chipped brick pathway to the rear, and down three steps to a wooden door whose well was deep in last year's leaves. From her pocket she pulled two keys and let them in.

"How come you have . . . ?"

"I told you it was my church," she said.

A flashlight sat in its box on the wall of the small vestibule; Lydia took it in her hand and closed and locked the door behind them: There they stood in close darkness, listening to the silence.

After a beat, she switched on the light and led him through a kitchen, across a large, desolate community room, still draped in streamers from the farewell party, its crepe once gay, now gray and ghostly in the shifting beam. Through a door and up a narrow stair, they emerged near the front of the sanctuary, lit now by the hueless, dingy window light. Lydia knelt and crossed herself, then led Julius down the central aisle to a place in the second row of pews, near the altar.

"The congregation moved," she said. "Merged. Over to Sullivan Street. The diocese couldn't afford the upkeep on two buildings. So now I'm the upkeep. Cheap. Free, in fact. I can't do much, but I do what I can."

Julius took her flashlight and examined the scene around him. Windows aside, it was truly quite clean, no dust, and not a spiderweb in sight. Above the altar, a man floated in the air.

"Who's that?" Pointing the flash.

"Joseph."

"Mary's Joseph?"

"Not *that* Joseph. Joseph of Cupertino."

"Silicon Valley?"

"Kingdom of Naples."

Julius examined the figure with the beam of light.

"What's he doing up in the air?"

"Whenever he felt ecstatic—and he often felt ecstatic—Joseph would levitate. Float up in the air, inches, feet, on good days to the top of the church."

"You're kidding."

"There were lots of witnesses. The congregation had to keep him under wraps so people wouldn't think it was the devil, or a stunt."

"When was this?"

"Seventeenth century. No magnetic beams. True rapture."

Julius could only shake his head. His light beam wandered the altar and froze on a painting behind it. He sprang from the pew to examine it more closely.

Feet. Vanishing. Into the clouds. The sinister, twisted, or clubbed. Horripilation.

"More Joseph?" Julius asked over his shoulder.

"The image of the disappearing Christ," she said, "the final moment of his human incarnation. 'And while they beheld, he was taken up; and a cloud received him out of their sight.' Acts 1:9."

"That's quite the act," Julius said as he rejoined her in the pew. The iambs of his footsteps drew attention to his limp.

"The last of the six leaps of Christ—from the incarnation to the ascension."

He who entered life through a slit in nature had left it by another.

Julius flicked off the switch to evade the aberrant. No light then, but rather darkness visible. The balustrade, the stonework, the stations of the cross. The organ, the stillness, the face of his beloved.

"Lydia . . ."

"Yes?"

"I know you must be judging me."

"I'm not."

"I wouldn't have gone along with just the Pentagon and K Street. Or even Earth's Friends. But the Church . . ."

"I understand."

"God is a no-man's land. . . ."

"I know."

"Everywhere is staggering disorder and affliction and stagnation. I thought we might find some secret . . . germ, something that could stay our murderous hands, that might blossom into a new Age of Faith. I was hoping for some light to fill the world across the nothingness, the terrible, universal malice."

"I know."

"Like when I first met you."

Something thonked against an eastern window and dropped into the yard—a rubber ball, a bird. . .

"The plane crash. Anyone. . ."

"No," he cut in. "My life—even then—was just . . . a hunger for some unfulfillable wish."

"Which is?"

"Consummation, unity, some all-encompassing embrace. I don't know. I confused that with you, with wanting you, with playing out our mammalian games."

"I thought we loved each other," she said.

"I was afraid of you, you know—bent over your Bible, brows knit, majestic, fierce. Your every movement seemed superior."

"Puppy love."

"Oh, no. Not at all. I watched you at the altar that first time in church. I watched you take God into your mouth, and I thought . . . I can't even say it. I wanted to . . . you know . . . and you said, 'I can't.' Not 'No,' not 'I don't want to,' not 'I'm too upset,' but 'I can't.' I hadn't realized I could have been your damnation. But then . . . remember standing there in front of that crèche, with the smell of pine trees, the shepherds . . . ?"

"I do."

"Everything I'd done till then was unfulfillment—and then, with you, a spontaneous coming-up, like a flock of birds in the fields. Everything I did was pulled upward."

Another soft thunk against the windows. Two. This time from the west. Then a crash and shattering of glass. Julius took the light, picked up a brick on the carpeted aisle, and made out the message scrawled across it.

"Does it say something?" Lydia asked.

"It says, 'THOU SHALT BE WITH ME IN HEAVEN.'"

A sparrow flew in through the broken window and fluttered around the beams, smashing repeatedly against the clerestory and landing at last on Saint Joseph's floating back.

"Kids," she said.

Not bloody likely.

They sat quietly again, though their heart rates may have matched the resting bird's.

"Lydia?"

"Yes?"

"I was grief-shaken when you left, confused, contrite. . . ."

"We were walking different ways."

“I know, I know, I know what we said: ‘Mine the church of saints, yours the church of sinners.’”

“You needed to stride ahead. I needed to kneel down. . . .”

“No, really, I . . .”

“Julius, it was right that we split. One tiny pain in the face of all the agony. . .”

Pock, thunk, pock, thwack, thump, pock, thump—mass suicide—a squadron of sparrows against the western windows. One made it through the jagged hole, ripping the feathers of its breast. It cried out loudly and grazed Julius’s head, flapping and dripping around the church, joining its fellow on Saint Joseph’s back before falling off that floating world onto the marble altar.

Julius began silently to weep. Lydia stood over him and dabbed his eyes with the hem of her t-shirt. He glimpsed her skin through blurring eyes, that belly, still taut, that had enticed and evaded.

Lydia walked slowly up to the altar—was she limping slightly?—and retrieved the bird. It lay in her hand still oozing blood from the laceration in its chest. Together they watched as it gave up its ghost. Though Julius could not, Lydia could see its spirit ascend. She laid her head back over the top of the pew and, through closed eyes, gazed beyond the vaulting roof.

“Let it go,” she said softly, to herself as much as to her friend. “Bring on the cloud of forgetting, and turn to the cloud of unknowing. . . .” Only her breath could be heard. *“Silentium mysticum . . . Silentium mysterium.”*

Lamentation on the Fall of a Sparrow

Magnified and sanctified may His great name be in the world that He created, as He wills.

In the darkness of that holy space under a floating Joseph, everything serious in human nature seemed called forth by the sublimation of that one small, winged creature.

And may His kingdom come in your lives and in your days and in the lives of all of the House of Israel, swiftly and soon, and say all Amen. May His great Name be blessed always and forever.

The ghostly stonework threw into contrast all in us that was compromised and dull, and created—in me, at least—a yearning to live up to its perfections.

Blessed and praised and glorified and raised and exalted and honored and uplifted and lauded be the Name of the Holy One. He is blessed above all blessings and hymns and praises and consolations that are uttered in the world, and say all Amen.

There *is* a special providence in the fall of a sparrow. For if it be now, 'tis not to come; if it be not to come, it will be now; if it be not now, yet it will come: the readiness is all.

May a great peace from heaven, and life, be upon us and upon all Israel, and say all Amen.

In the semidark, I inspected the bird in Lydia's hand. The gash in its chest smiled at me with the soft red lips of an awaiting friend.

May He who makes peace in His high places make peace upon us and upon all Israel, and say all Amen.

14.

Hysterica Passio

My father died a child," she said, bird in hand, her eyes still closed. "Last week. He was ninety-two."

"I'm sorry."

"He lay there with an old man's beard on a young man's face, handsome, even dead, brilliant, funny, looking a little embarrassed. You know what I asked him?"

"No."

"'So why did you live?'"

"What did he say?"

"Nothing."

She placed the bird on the cushion at her side. Julius turned it so it wouldn't stain.

"I also thought about you," she said, her eyes opening, looking at the blood on her hands. "I wasn't lonesome before I met you. Then I was. You brought me alive."

Julian moved closer and took her reddened hand in his.

"You got me started filmmaking."

"I did? You didn't even own a camera when we. . ."

"All those Chaplin films you took me to. At the Catholic Worker, I was inspired to make my own versions."

"The documentaries."

"Yes. *Tramp*—about the friends I made at hospitality house. Then *Modern Times* . . ."

"I saw that. About the Stevens workers."

"Then *City Lights* and *The Gold Rush*."

"Didn't see those. Are you still making them?"

"After *The Great Dictator*, I couldn't get funding. . . . Yiii!"

She jumped as if nicked by a stun gun.

"What's wrong?"

"Nothing. Just cramps."

Julius reached out to her. She pushed his hand away.

"I made those films—me with Kropotkin—then down to D.C. with Newsreel. . . . The sadness of sin out there, the unspeakable dreariness . . . To try to nourish the Catholic Worker world—a society where it's easier for people to be good. The old Wobbly dream—to build a new society within the shell of the old.

"Then one day I noticed I couldn't take a joke anymore. I couldn't even see straight with the dust in my eyes blowing from Laos and Cambodia and Vietnam. Our whole nation completely pathological. Archbishop Romero killed. The Contras. No one was Thou—everyone was It. I couldn't love a country which might be destroyed, or any city which could be turned to rubble. And worse, I couldn't love a person who could kill or be killed, and that was everyone. And you saved me again."

"Me? I'd lost track of you completely."

"It's stupid, but in my heart I connected you with Julian of Norwich."

"The 'all-will-be-well-again' guy?"

"Except she wasn't a guy, Julius. She was a nun with visions. I picked up her work—*Showings*—on Fourth Avenue. Twenty-five cents. I thought it was a cheap photography book. It changed my life."

Julian waited.

"It showed me about justice and mercy and the suffering of the innocent. 'All is Love,' she said. In my head, it was as if *you* said it. Julius-Julian. People suffer when they can't remain in love at the core. And then there's so much sorrow—existing apart from God, from Love. Insufficiency, contingency, incompleteness, mortality, self-forgetting. She gave me a vision of love and work, and passion for life.

"I went back to the hospitality houses with new determination. Julius, can you understand this?" She sat up straight and turned directly to him.

"The poor and oppressed are collectively the Messiah," she said. "You get it? *They* are the Messiah. They bring us the Beatitudes. So I don't want just missionary people like the Salvation Army to be kind to the poor. I want *everyone* to learn from them. I want every home open to the lame and the blind, the way it is after earthquakes and floods—when people really live, really love their brothers and sisters. That's what I want.

"I know it's not realistic. I don't care. Everyone needs a sense of guilt, responsibility, an understanding that they're privileged, living on others."

"Sometimes the poor can be beasts," Julius said.

"Then we should *comfort* the beastly. And feed the hungry, and clothe the naked, shelter the homeless, ransom the captive, visit the sick, bury the dead."

"Do you still film them?"

"No. I sold my equipment. You do these things blindly, you know, not because you really want to, but because you want to live in conformity with the will of God, in a community of God."

Julius was saddened by old distances invading once again. He wanted to draw her to him, but like the black and white Scotties, he couldn't get past the force.

"That God tolerates the Church amazes me," he said. "The empty ritual by people who pretend to know what they're doing . . ."

She closed her eyes and took a quick, deep breath, as if in pain. Julius watched her with cathode concentration. She sighed and looked at him.

"Hell," she said, "is the place where no order is."

Once again, she looked old to him, not as before, in simple contrast with earlier memories, but genuinely aged.

"Faith is a talent," Julius said, "a gift I don't have. I can only keep searching."

"You wouldn't seek Him if you hadn't already found Him."

They sat in silence for several minutes, she with her head back over the pew, breathing slowly and deeply, he watching her, his breath rapid and shallow—until she stopped it with a sudden kiss.

"It's the Fall," she said. Julius did not understand. "The apple gravitating toward the animal—something a physicist might understand?"

She closed her eyes again, this time so close to his face. She sang, Gregorian:

O quam mirabilis est praescientia divini pectoris
quae praescivit omnem creaturum.

Julius remembered that angelic soprano voice, rising so strangely from her deeper alto. As ever, he felt disabled by the magic flow of chant tones, engaged at a level where his intellect could only stand dumb, overwhelmed by a spiritual sound-force which laid his soul bare as did nothing else in the human plane.

"It's wrong," she stopped and said. "It's wrong to think so much about human love. *God* is all, and love is only love of God."

She gave a shudder. Her face grimaced. She closed her eyes and waited for it to pass.

"Why am I trapped inside this body?" she blurted out, her words echoing off stone. And then she loudly groaned and stood up slowly. She moved in front of Julius in the narrowness of the pew.

"Hoc est corpus meus," she whispered as she lifted the front of her shirt. NOTRE DAME, it said. Over her bra she lifted it, over her ample breasts, and held it with her chin.

"*Hoc est corpus,* hocus-pocus, hocus-pocus," she chanted softly, chuckling. She unhitched the hook and opened herself to the man she had so long denied, burying his face deep between her breasts as if she would replace her very heart with his pulsing skull.

They stretched out on the softly cushioned pew and laughed and cried, and gasped and sighed, and liquid flowed in both, and *consummatum est.* In the quiet of postcoital breathing, a soft beating of wings.

"I *believe* in angels," she murmured.

As it grew louder, Julius and Lydia knew it for what it was. They both jumped up and into a wretched imitation of propriety.

The wings beat hard at the eastern windows.

"Lady and gentleman," the loudspeaker blared, "please be advised that the Hound of Heaven Helicopter is here, with Operation Flaming Sword. You have five minutes to clear the premises. This is your final warning." And the archangel made off heavenward, to hover and wait.

They fled through the dark basement rooms, avoiding the east, feinting to the west and north, and returned *chez elle,* like the Magi, by another way.

What they missed were the pamphlets dropped at the main entrance, their assumed exit.

WE HAVE NOT LEARNED ANYTHING, they said.

WE DON'T KNOW ANYTHING,

WE DON'T HAVE ANYTHING,

WE DON'T UNDERSTAND ANYTHING,

WE DON'T SELL ANYTHING,

WE DON'T HELP,

WE DON'T BETRAY,

AND WE WILL NOT FORGET.

What they also missed was the flight of Saint Joseph, from over the altar to under the rafters, and all around the church.

ZAYIN

The Doodad Imagined

He had told her of his accident, of the MRI, and the genesis of the Doodad. But what did he tell her? God's laws, like Murphy's, work in mysterious ways. And most every silver lining has its cloud. How had he hit upon the Doodad? By being hit upon by a huge boulder advancing up at him at 32 feet/sec^2, on a mountainside in Maine.

"Marantz . . ."

A very arrogant leper, a high-handed leper, with leprous head in clouds. He thought he thought he was a Jew

"You had a fall when you were

non serviam, he

"Katahdin

remain alive at any price

"neck

The Lord Is Risen from Chaos and Old Night

“here

the unhandseled globe

“helicopter

The fall, the fall, the fall of God most holy

“Bangor

until it gives way to the back, *beyond* back, resurrection with no glory

“it seems

tapering always downward in the funnel, the blueprints of hell

“hit your head and

like a moth to a flame, connected by the magnetic

“Mr. Marantz, do your eyes hurt?”

10/13/90

S:43 yo white male, Katahdin fall, approx 30 feet, 48 hours ago. Friends report loss of consciousness, ’30 minutes. Pt backboarded, leg fx splinted, medivacked to EMMC, admitted 10/12/87, 15:30h. Limb x-rayed, casted; CT for head injury; C-spine x-rays suspicious for ligamentous injury. See admissions note.

O: Vital signs stable

Gen: Arouses to painful stim—mumbles unintelligible words. Moves all 4s purposefully.

HEENT: Pupils equal, round, reactive to light

Neck: in C collar

Lungs: Clear to auscultation

CV: Regular rate, rhythm, without murmurs, rubs, gallops.

Abd: soft, +bowel sounds

Extremities: L distal tib fx, casted, +sensation, +cap refill, congenital deformity—missing distal R foot; otherwise WNL

A/P: #1 CNS—R/O bleed by CT yesterday. Concussion. Will follow mental status.

#2 C-spine. Some evidence of laxity on C-spine x-rays yesterday. No fx seen. Will MRI neck to R/O ligamentous injury.

#3 tibial fx, splinted, doing well

P. Gunther, MD

"Mr. Marantz . . ."

"Mmmm . . ."

"set you up for an MRI to look at your neck."

dim brain, half-spoken words. Will you save me? Ah, something laughed.

"painless

"Uh-hmm."

“about an hour

What business have I with Heaven? The old knowledge. A slow creature among light creatures. My whole life spreads surf like sea foam.

“sliding table

Was it worth it to die on the cross if this is what exists—the earth irredeemably condemned, buzzards above? There may be nothing left to learn. The old knowledge. Now, this is it, said Death. Today, perhaps, I'll give up living.

From morn
To noon he fell, from noon to dewy eve,
A summer's day; and with the setting Sun
Dropp'd from the Zenith like a falling Star—

“state of the art

a place both very near and very far—the other side of life

“surface coil positioned around your head

the foot is more wicked than the rest of the body because it is farther from heaven

“see and hear you

spoken of, not with

“music if you

What music? Every sickness a musical problem, and every cure a musical solution. Shadows creeping in. When I was sinking down, sinking down, sinking down . . . Rest of their bones, and soul's delivery “loud knocking sounds

a constant pestering in my ears, a moth perhaps, the buzz of flies, and then a limping drum. Proximity. Who is that peering at me? Why? A small seed of death, perhaps, stuck on my cheek? Rotting? Death, wing thyself away from me, that in my veins red life may stream again.

“kind of magnetize you

the black mountains, the castle of Asmodeus, and fallen off the edge of the world

“protons are first ‘excited’ and then ‘relaxed’

forced to marry a demon princess

“you may notice a warm feeling

“sequences

Lydia, you’ve come

“lie very still. . . . have any questions?”

oasis

“Boy, I did Katahdin once,” the doctor said, mustachioed.

“Yeah?”

“Man, what a climb! There’s about a mile of the regular stuff in from the trail head, the usual forest hike. But then, Jesus, up we go—five miles, five thousand vertical feet, *up*, all rock and all up. Huge boulders everywhere, a trail winding up over piles and piles of rocks. You need both hands to climb—every finger and muscle. That’s where he fell—just before you hit Thoreau Spring.”

"Mountain Rescue report?"

"No, his friends. Up on the summit there are amazing views in every direction. Phil took some pictures I can show you. I'll bring 'em tomorrow. Coming down was way more frightening—you know, looking down? I had to face the rock to keep from getting vertigo."

"Mr. Marantz? MR. MARANTZ?"

"Unh."

"Mr. Marantz? Can you hear me?"

"Um."

"We're going to take you in now for the MRI. You still there?"

"Unh."

"It's a fun trip. No pain. Worst may be the noise, but you can listen to music or . . ."

"Unh-uh."

"OK. Whatever. You've been cleared by x-ray for metal. Wouldn't want that old shrapnel to come tearing out of you. . . ."

"Unh-unh."

There are men who would open what is closed. There are men who would open anything, men who would open men to see

"You still with us?"

"Yes. Yes."

"Hey! Is that your first word? Real word? Good one! Right through here. Thar she blows."

A magnet hung in a hardware shop. Scary-looking. Yes. Terrifying. But alluring, alluring, O Imp of Perversity. Swallow me whole.

"It's a remarkable piece of apparatus."

"Um."

"Very ingenious. Quite the doodad."

"Siemens," Julius noted.

"Nothing but the best."

"Jewish slaves."

"What?"

"They used slave labor. . . ."

"OK, let's get you onto the table. Easy does it, watch the neck. Ronnie, grab the cast. . . ."

Into the throbbing womb, out of the too-bright light, the artificial air and light.

"Comfy?"

"Not bad."

"Told you so. OK, see right up there's the microphone and the speakers. You can always talk to us in the control room anytime. Can you fold your hands over your chest?"

Like death. Peace. Like Mom and Dad, like death.

"Good. So we're going to do some sequences with different intervals. That's when you'll hear the knocking. We'll tell you how long before each one. Want some music?"

"No."

"Don't like music, huh? Me neither. Too much music in the

world today, I say. So you'll just put up with the noise. If you change your mind, give a yell, and we'll set you up with earphones. I'm going into that room. See, behind the glass? You hang in there. The first interval will be forty-five seconds. Hold still, now."

And? And? Suspended in silence on polished steel? An alien abduction? Breathe?

The rat-a-tat-tatting began, harrowing. A man disappeared, lashed by nothingness, transposed into sound, the mighty wind that is the Wrath of God. Unaccustomed superimposition of planes. And then silence.

As if I were turned off. Blessed release.

"Good one. You did fine. OK, next one's longer. Three minutes this time. Think you can deal?"

"Mm."

"Can't hear you."

"Yes."

"All right, here we go."

A loud knocking this time, Niebelungen nightmare. Flonkflonk-flonkflonkflonk. And a nausea came over him, fusing of brain with world, acquiescing to mute, motionless force, motionless, directed force. Drawn to you like moth to flame.

Then—the dawn of blue-eyed days, a scattering, like sand, like foam.

"Good going, Mr. Marantz. Didn't hurt, did it? Give us a minute, here, relax. OK, this is the biggie. We're goin' for broke. Fifteen minutes. Just hang in there."

Bonkabonkabonkabonkabonka.

Upward extrusion. Flashing gleams of life. Power like a paw coursing through the earth and him, raking him straight with its talons. Wrath-fire. It is a fearful thing to fall into the hands of the living God.

Bonkabonkabonka.

Completeness, proportion infusing his being, a glimpse beyond the horizon, with brain swelling through galaxies, motionless writhing, ecstatic, devotional merging.

Bonkabonkabonkabonkabonkabonkabonka.

Mysterium tremendum, stipiosum et alienum. The hundred-letter word flattening him out, perfectly collapsed, perfectly extended, thin as paper, pledged to muteness under brazen excitation, the furious energy, the open noise of agony, his breaths forming a dotted line, asserting their nothingness against a force, his blood becoming white, his embers dilating, tearing, his voice a thin silence, drawn, drawn, drawn toward and drawn away.

Bonkabonkabonk.

Silence.

And he cleared the whirring edge, the heaves of storm. And he did not weigh a gram. And he rode the downwind from the open grave above, back into a world more blue than blue. Scattered like sand he was, like foam, fondled by love-fire on being's beach, inversion layer, existence dispossessed.

I gave it all my strength, he thought. *It gave me all its strength, but that strength may be too great.*

"Excellent. I think we've got what we need."

He lay in the coffin of the magnet, shattered, yet having shed his husks, the shells of his enigma.

This was what he told her—and didn't.

Outside, that day, others in white coats discovered holes in the ozone, the President compared the contras to the Founding Fathers, and a Japanese 747 crashed into a mountain, killing 520 in the worst air accident ever.

And after a week, Julius returned to his lab.

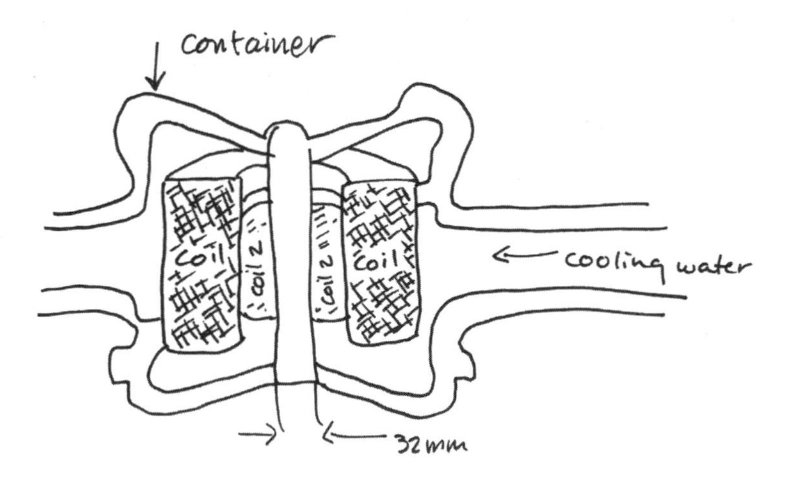

(SKETCH FROM JULIUS MARANTZ'S LAB NOTEBOOK 7, 3/18/93)

He started with tubes, of course, inducing magnetism in diamagnetic objects far smaller than himself. At 100,000 gauss (10 teslas), using classical double-solenoid design, he was able to suspend small pieces of bismuth and tin in a stable zone toward the top of the bore.

His colleagues were amazed, for there is a widespread assumption that only a very few materials, such as iron and nickel, are strongly magnetic, while most are not—or at least only one-billionth as much. But they were wrong, victims of unthinking tradition and suffering from Aristotelian stiff-neckedness. They were taken in by two counterintuitive facts, each convincingly coiled within the other: one, the magnetic field actually required to lift a piece of iron is just a few gauss, much less than the output of the lifting magnet; and two, the lifting power of the magnetic field increases as the square of its value. Given the readjustment of all electron orbits in magnetic fields, and the sum of billions upon billions of them in all objects, most objects, even "nonmagnetic" ones, are diamagnetic and can be lifted. This he showed, early on, and was able to claim the Babson money to start the Middlebury Mag Lab.

Tiny pieces of nonferrous metals, small graphite beads, and droplets of water or acetone were one thing: larger objects required stronger magnetic fields. Julius plunged headlong into magnetic theory and design and came up with significant advances—primarily to the cooling system—on the magnet conceived in 1939 by Francis Bitter at MIT.

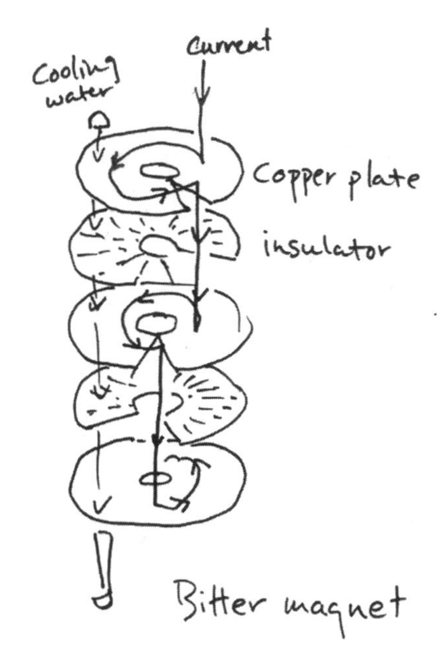

(SKETCH FROM JULIUS MARANTZ'S LAB NOTEBOOK 7, 7/20/93)

Julius's "windings" were sets of thin conducting plates, each like a big washer, slit along a radius. In each plate, a voltage difference between the two edges of the slit forced the current to flow circumferentially before entering the next plate via the axial clamping. His design had many virtues, possessing great inherent strength and permitting the use of a wide range of conductors, with a favorable cooling geometry enabling his magnets to absorb high power densities.

By 1994, using Bitter-Marantz magnets and a good deal of Babson money, he was able to attain fields of 12 to 14 T and thus to levitate larger objects: frog's eggs, blueberries, strawberries, hazelnuts, cherry tomatoes, and small pieces of pizza.

In 1998, his work took a fateful turn. Thinking back to his initial experiments, Julius wondered how frog's eggs might develop after being exposed to strong magnetic fields. Instead of just tossing his tiny subjects, he allowed them to develop. Tadpoles and adults all were normal, morphologically and behaviorally, and could reproduce in turn. Which led Julius to levitating those tadpoles and, with fields of 15 to 16T, adult frogs. The frogs would swim around in the air at the top of Julius's solenoids for as long as thirty minutes, and after reorienting from zero gravity seemed no worse for wear, happily joining their fellow frogs in a biology department terrarium.

From frogs to mice, from mice to kittens, from kittens to . . . nowhere. Julius's magnets gave up after kittens. He needed another design. After a postdoc year at the National High Magnetic Field Laboratory at Los Alamos, he was ready to get beyond solenoids into external fields, focused by magnetic lenses. He was ready for the Doodad.

He was not ready for all that followed.

15.

Not Despisèd but Rejected: GEKO Closes In

Back in her apartlet, Lydia dropped into a chair.

"I can't do it, Julius—even if you buy the camera."

"But they're taking over the world, duping everyone, murdering people left and right. . . ."

"All will be well," she insisted. "'Alle shalle be wele, and alle shalle be wele, and alle maner of thynge shalle be wele.'"

"How do *you* know? When? What about the people suffocating in the troposphere, icing in the stratosphere, decomposing in the Van Allen belt? Is all well with them?"

"You're going to have another panic attack."

"Damn right I am—'cause you won't help me. You're the last of my resources."

"I *am* helping you. I'm trying to. I'm telling you to back off. Tell them you'll keep quiet. Yes, people are dying, Yes, they're targeted by evil phonies. But alle shalle be wele. This moment is part of God's desires. . . ."

"How do you know anything about God's desires? Perhaps He wants something else entirely—or nothing!"

"Julius, this is a teaching time. You can't demand a total solution for the world—everyone is guilty."

"Some more than others!"

"We're all His creatures. You think Christ came down once and for all, for no reason? You think He ascended once and for all, and pulled up his cross behind him? He's been rising for two thousand years, transforming consciousness. Hope has grown, courage, a sense of sacrifice and reverence among millions of people."

"What good does that do the raptured?"

"You can't just see existence in terms of individual lives."

"Bullshit!"

"That's Julian's theodicy . . ."

"The-idiocy!"

". . . Evil does not exist. Get it? Get it?" Lydia demanded. "Evil does not exist."

"You believe alle is fucking wele? This is a world of endless outrages, Lydia, where children kill children. This is a world that shows God's fangs! How should I trust Him?"

"How can we *not* trust Him?"

Julius collapsed on the couch.

"Hopeless. You're hopeless."

She brought him a warm glass of Calmex™, sat down, and rubbed his back while he drank.

"You know what I think?" she said. "The secret of life is to act as though we have whatever we most lack. That's the whole doctrine of Christianity. Convincing ourselves that everything is created for the good, that the brotherhood of man really exists. . . . And if it's not true, so what? It's believing it that counts, not whether it's real.

"Don't focus on the cause of evil, Julius. Look at its ultimate consequences—God's repair of the world. Mr. Fixit bigger than your dad. It would be awful if in this . . . this phony life where there's so little to love, our souls would stop loving. Then God's absence would be final. All we *have* to do is to go on loving in the darkness—"

He watched her quivering. He handed her his empty glass.

"So you won't help me," he said.

Again she winced, as at the church, and took a breath, and sighed.

"More cramps?"

She nodded.

He rubbed her abdomen, as she had rubbed his back. Now touching was allowed—a small great joy even in despair. It was time for the angel to come.

It came as before, descending obtusely from a distant heaven, a crescendo in quantized steps, in teasing terraced dynamics: wa wa wa wa Wa Wa Wa Wa WA WA WA WA WA WA WA WA.

WAAAt in me is dark

Illumine, it said,

What is low raise and support;

That to the height of this great argument

I may assert eternal Providence

And justify the ways of God to men.

It said.

On came the Anthrax at 110 decibels, the sound level of a riveter. The same track as was used on Noriega.

I AM THE LAW

And you won't fuck around no more

WA WA WA WA WA WA WA

Textured around and within it were the screams of multitudes, the sound of seven thunders, and the howl of dragons. A great voice from Heaven sang at 115 decibels:

Because in Megacity

I AM THE LAW

WA WA WA WA WA WA WA WA WA WA

Stomp, stomp, stomp, the idiot convention

Had enough, Marantz?

Alabama was barking, fast and crazy. Lydia wrapped a pillow around her head and ran into the sleeping cubby.

The decibels went to 120, the level of a thunderclap directly overhead, but constant.

I'm trying to reason but you don't understand.

WA WA WA WA WA WA WA WA WA WA

Come out, Mr. Marantz. Come out now.

Loud cries, harpers harping, lions roaring, sounds of horses. The air was filled with Exxon.

WA WA WA WA WA WA WA WA Wa Wa Wa Wa wa wa wa wa

And then there was silence in heaven for about the space of half an hour.

Lydia would not come out of the cubby. Twenty minutes of Julius's gentle ministrations—but she just lay there and sobbed. Heaven-deafened, bootless cries; she'd broken like a scrannel pipe of straw. Wretched. And wretched.

Julius thought it best to leave, to move his danger out from under. She will recover, he thought—she always does.

Down the stairs, past the guys, checking the alleys of sky above, alert for the beating of wings, over to Canal Street, and down the steps to the IND. He waited, yet unharmed, for the southbound A train.

Shame on his heart for beating the quarter notes of Mingus and the Duke:

If two three four one *you miss the A train* three four one two three four

You'll two *find* four one *you missed the quickest way to Harlem.*

• • •

Was *Dasein* so frivolous as to chant ditties in a time of greatest need?

It is said, "A Christian is a person whose death is behind him." Maybe that was it. In any case, and strangely enough, Julius Marantz was off—for the first time in years—to Coney Island.

Magnified and sanctified may His great name be in the world that He created, as He wills.

16.

In the Lydian Mode

Unseen by Julius, but sitting open on the counter during his visit was the surgery/pathology report from Lydia's surgery, three weeks prior:

> Poorly differentiated adenocarcinoma of the right ovary, with extensive peritoneal seeding and metastases to 8 of 17 lymph nodes. Center of the tumor necrotic and deeply ulcerated.

She had of course refused chemotherapy and radiation, preferring to accept the will of God. At the time of Julius's visit, she was using only Gulf/Sonoco Gold™ for pain control.

Progression was predictable and uninhibited. Liver involvement swelled her abdomen and yellowed her skin. She developed blockage of her bowels with severe abdominal pain and vomiting. Her right leg became swollen from pressure on the femoral vein, and as other invaded vessels and organs became obstructed, her biochemistry became deranged. God's music here was a concerto grosso, featuring what the eighteenth-century pathologist Giovanni Morgagni called "the cries of the suffering organs," and cadencing one month later in cachexia and death.

If what Julius didn't know didn't hurt him, other things did.

Lamentation on the Love of Death and the Death of Love

She will recover. She always does. But I will not. I feel the chill of death.

Death will be relief from pain, but mostly from monotony. The struggle has become too tedious to go on.

The world is bent on suicide: whatever is, is wrong; history stays centrifugal. My melancholy task, I see, is unperformable. What a long, long learning! Why evade the final lesson?

Love. An especially nasty kind of injury to one's narcissism. The two of us huffing and puffing in a pew, pretending to be alive. Love. Its outcome? Nothing. No child produced, no relationship attained, no product, no film even, to document the truth. An affirmation, yes, but of ephemera.

Beauty has its secrets, yes, and some are like a hand that strangles. Love will continue without Venus, and war without Mars. A dim consolation: one day, even the sun will perish.

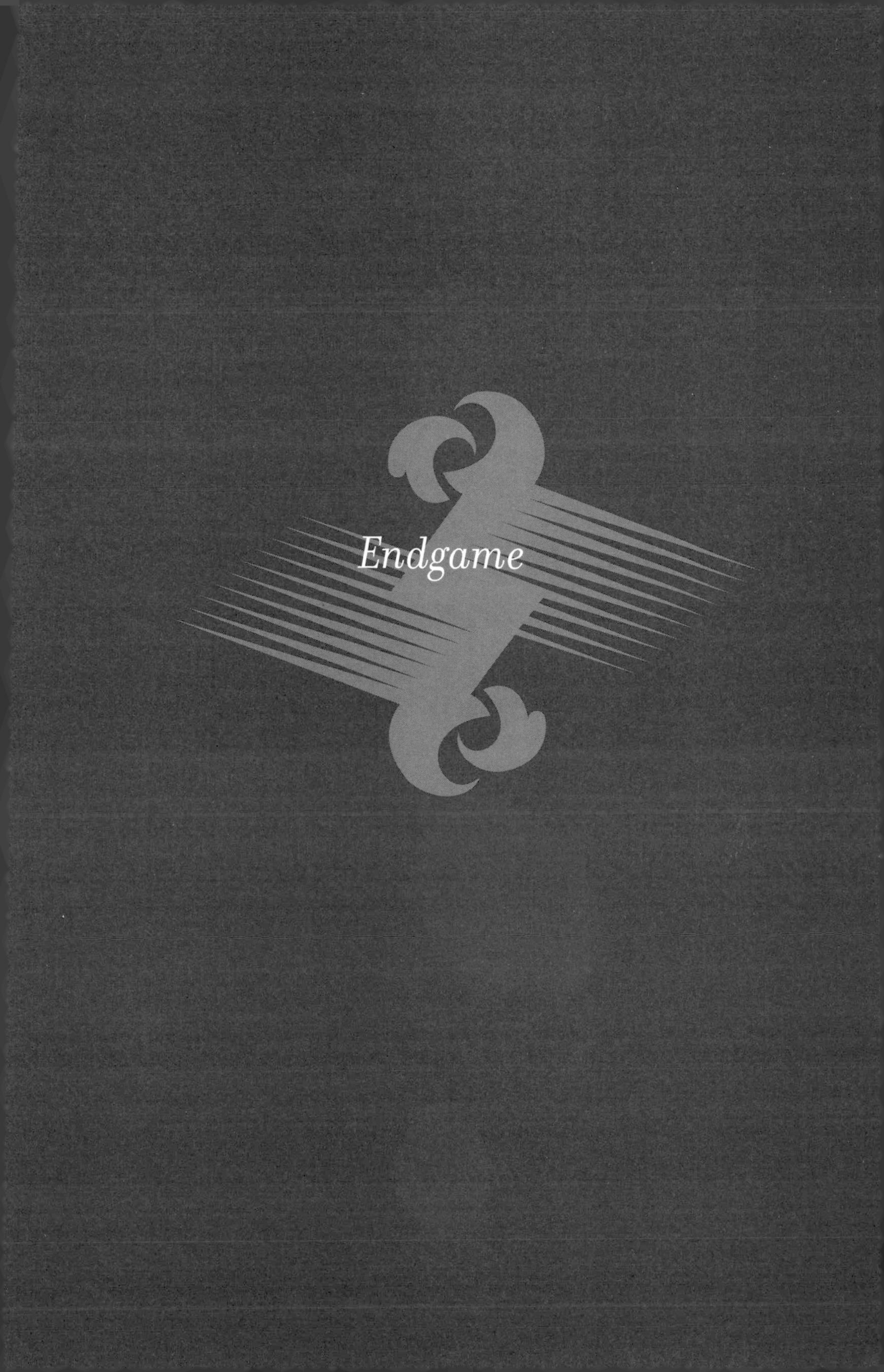

Endgame

17.

Babylon Is Fallen

Julius Marantz was off—for the first time in years—to Coney Island. But not before heading three blocks south, to stand for a moment at Ground Zero.

He felt less frantic now, in this hole, this pit. It *was* a sacred place, just as they said, almost a Kiva, in which to contemplate great pillars of Injustice. Plus God had once made everything out of nothing, and here, above all, ur-nothingness showed through.

Perhaps nothingness was in the minds of the designers of the holographic monument, currently performing its daytime flow of images. Performance, performance, performance. Location, location, location. Perhaps it was simply to save insurance companies the reconstruction funds and shift the burden onto taxpayer energy costs. Whatever the motivation, the result was a monument both to patriotism and to science.

Julius watched, transfixed as the third image of the America Triumphs Trinity cross-faded with the first: DreamWorks' twenty-billion-dollar "safe and reliable"® mushroom cloud was rising off into space, dissolving in gorgeous corporate images consistent with flag version 52.8. Red, white, and blue over green. The greening of the earth, the greening of the sky.

Rising under the cloud's upward disappearance, a 1,776-foot flagpole was laboriously raised east to west from its bed along Vesey Street by four thirty-five-story U.S. Marines in an astounding animation sequence based on Joe Rosenthal's famous photo from Iwo Jima. With this image, Gigantorama had won a Gemmy for biggest holograph of 2002. At its top, a 900-by–500-foot Old Glory fluttered in the wind, even on the calmest days, its photons caressing buildings near and far.

After persisting for its scheduled five minutes, Iwo Jima morphed into Fox News' winner—the triumphant exit from Saigon, Americans atop the Hilton being ferried away by a fleet of angel helicopters, rotors replaced by feathery wings to heavenly strains from *Lohengrin*. After five minutes of such transport, the mushroom cloud bloomed once again.

The images were frankly awesome. The reference beam must have been projected from the General Dynamics satellite, Julius imagined, and the object beam from—where?—likely the new Building Seven, almost rebuilt. The amount of energy used for the lasers must have been stupendous, but no more, he figured, than that spent on the raptures.

In this magical space, images bubbled up from other worlds. The desperate public ideas concerning the building collapses. Lunatic, he thought. The world in denial. America needs steel to melt at kerosene temperatures, and floors to pancake through a hundred floors that offer no resistance. Better embrace the implausible than admit the obvious. And Building Seven in front of him. No planes, no significant fires, and still it fell at free-fall speed, symmetrically.

Oh well, nothing to be done except get rid of the evidence and silence all the whistleblowers. Nothing to be done.

Whiffs of his old life floated by, reminders of a past identity. How easy it had been for Philippe and him, and Jean-François and Jean-Louis, to sneak into a closed area, to lug hundreds of pounds of equipment to the roof of the buildings. . . . Playful, they had been, kids, idealistic, not like . . . Julius thought of the many GEKOs before his GEKO, the great hidden histories not taught in schoolbooks. We'll need a new Pearl Harbor, they wrote.

The graffiti on the fence said, LOVE IS GONE, BUT WAR REMAINS. And the composer of this world was not Monteverdi but Mantovani. How hard then to understand the plot, the plotted, plotting plot, God's or GEKO's, the way things work.

Because once you realized how things worked, you could fill in the blanks, Mendeleev deducing the periodic table of the elements, then searching to see if there were actual elements that fit.

Nothing to be done.

Pessimism of the intellect, optimism of the will. Reason versus Faith.

A busload of tourists from Kansas, all outfitted with American-flag baseball caps and I♥NY tees, unloaded and snapped away.

Some even took pictures of Julia to chuckle over with their friends at home.

He didn't care. He felt light. He felt he needed the entire force of gravity to keep him on the earth.

His faith?

Speckl'd vanity will sicken soon and die,
and leprous sin will melt from earthly mould,
and Hell itself will pass away,
and leave her dolorous mansions to the peering day.

Alle shalle be wele, and alle shalle be wele, and alle maner of thynge shalle be wele.

Julius took the IND at the newly restored World Trade Center station and headed out toward Brooklyn.

18.

The Final Lesson

Change for the F at Jay Street/Borough Hall. Julius located the correct stairwell and began limping the two flights down.

In the middle of the platform on the F-train level, the Stygian Wings Theater Association was set up to perform: two poles in cement blocks with a cross-pole tied between them, the funky frame supporting a canvas flip-chart on which was painted

THE KANTISTORIA OF SAINT JULIUS

THE HOSPITABLE

by G. FLOWBEAR

Under a charming rendering of Grateful Dead dancing bears, skull-angels bore the following subepigraph:

Two things fill the mind with ever-increasing wonder and awe: the starry sky above, and the moral law within.

—IMMANUEL KANT

The entire Stygian company consisted of one red-haired, strong-toothed puppeteer, with cymbal and horn attached to a bass drum, the player wielding a soft mallet as baton, pointer, and musical weapon. Spying Julius coming down the stairs, he announced in stentorian voice: "At last, at last, ladies and gentlemen, at last we can begin."

He beckoned Julius around to the front of the gathered crowd, pointing out the correspondence between the title of the show and what might be Julius's name. Performances, performances, performances. Yet another. Suspicious but intrigued, Julius cautiously obeyed. Mr. Stygian waited for the southbound local to pull out and dissolve into remembered sound. And then. . .

"Ladies and gentlemen, a feeble, the Legend of Saint Julius the Hospitable. Are you ready?"

General assent.

BOOM BOOM

He flipped the cover canvas over behind the cross-pole, and revealed nine squares, two feet by two feet, three across and three down. painted in primary colors on a field of fluorescent green. As he recited his text, he pointed with mallet to the paintings and their details.

"*Der var engang en lille Barn, saa fin og saa nydelig,* and his name was Julius.

CLASH

"His mother and father lived in a land by the edge of the sea. And by dint of their prayers,

TOOT TOOT

a son was born to them.

"And at his birth, an angel came to his mother in a moonbeam CLASH and whispered, 'Rejoice, oh Mom. Your son shall be a saint.'

"'Feh,' she said, 've don't got saints,' she said. 'All right,' said the angel, 'a zaddik, then.'

BOOM

"And to his father, the angel whispered, 'His foot shall be the mark of hidden glory.'

“Therefore they named him for a king, and had kingly dreams for him. To make him brave, his father took him flying.

SIREN WHISTLE

“At tournaments he always won the prize; his little subjects—hamsters, mice, a mother’s gut, and ondts—were not as pleased as he. Their writhings

THUMP THUMP THUMP

made his heart thump.

CLASH

“His faithful Yenta barked at him, ‘Accursed boy, *scientium,* so vain and self-important, one day you shall scarab your parents. Ruf ruf!”

"'No, no,' said Julius—and sent them off to their deaths.

TAPS.

Razor blades? An accident?

"Aghast, repentant, taking up the cross, globetrotting, gracehopping, he climbed and climbed until he fell. BOOM.

"He fell into the vibrationally satanic, into the arms of those who would embrace him."

BOOM BOOM BOOM BADABABOOM

Stygian kept up his drumming through the approach and unloading of the uptown local across the tracks. He flipped the chart to the second set of nine.

CLASH

"People died because of Julius. What would it take to learn?

CYMBALS BANGED AGAINST THE HEAD

"Repentant yet again, afraid for others, he fled from men and lived on roots and berries in a squalid hut.

LOUD CHEWING ON CARROT PULLED FROM POCKET

"For years he lived alone, never seeing another person, until one midwinter evening he returned home to find a man sitting on his stool, wrapped in a tattered tallis, his face a mask, his eyes redder than coals.

TICKS ON CYMBAL

Coming closer with his lantern, Julius saw a hideous Leper.

CLASH

No nose had he, but just a hole, and his breath was thick and nauseous. "Oi, I am hungry," said the Leper. Julius gave him what he had—some crusts of black bread.

BOOM

"'I am so toisty.' He stretched out his arm, and with one gulp downed the cup of water he was offered.

BOOM

"'I am *kalt.* I am soooo tired.' His ulcers began to ooze. *'Dein bett,'* the Leper murmured, and Julius helped him onto the mattress and covered him with the rags he used for blankets.

"'It is like *ice* in *mein* bones,' he said. 'Come close to *mir.*' And Julius lay down on the covers beside him.

"'No. *Unter.* Come *unter* and varm me,' the Leper said. 'Undress, and gif me the varmth of *dein körper.*'

CYMBAL TREMOLO

Julius took off his clothing and lay down under the covers. He felt the leprous skin touching his thigh, colder than a serpent and rough as a file. Infectious."

The downtown F approached in gradual crescendo.

"'Come closer and varm me more. More than *dein* hends. Varm me with *dein ganzer körper.*' And Julian stretched himself mouth to mouth, breast to breast."

Disgusted, attracted, wanting to stay but needing to go, Julius backed toward the slowing train.

"Watch the doors, watch the doors," the loudspeakers crackled. Stygian watched Julius enter the car. He watched the doors close. He watched Julius watch him through the window. The train pulled slowly out and shrank away down the Cimmerian track.

"So what happened? What happened?" some children asked. The ending was played for the crowd alone.

"The Leper embraced him.

SOFT CLASH

With eyes become clear as stars and hair like solar rays. Julius breathed in the rose-fragrance of his breath, enraptured in a superhuman joy.

CYMBAL TREMOLO AND CRESCENDO

His lover grew until his head and feet touched the walls of the hut. The roof flew off, the firmament opened

CLASH

—and Julian ascended toward the blue, face to face with One who bore him away."

The puppeteer smiled with strong teeth, bowed, and elicited ambivalent applause. As the crowd dispersed, hoping to avoid his passed top hat, he called after them: "Jesus Christ may be a great lord, but he will not keep company with others. He is proud and needs to rule the earth. Be careful before you honor him."

He boarded the uptown express, having collected some three dollars and change.

HETH

A Study of History

Look homeward, Angel, now and melt with ruth; ruth, in this case, being not an old girlfriend, but a Miltonic state of pity and compassion, sorrow, grief, remorse, and lamentation. Such was Julius's state as he subwayed and elevated his way back to where he'd started, to know the place, perhaps, for the first time, the end of his exploring.

Coney Island . . .

Prospect Park, Fort Hamilton, Church and Ditmas . . .

Whither runneth my sweetheart?
Whither runneth my sweetheart?
Stay, stay, stay, stay
And take me with you.

Varm me with *dein ganzer körper.*

Avenue I . . . Avenue N . . . Avenue U . . . Avenue X . . .

Watch the doors, watch the doors.

I am hungry. I am *kalt.* I am sooo tired.

Hey ding a ding a ding, hey ding a ding a ding

Neptune Avenue

I thought I should please thee ere we did part.

Last stop, Stillwell Avenue, Coney Island. Watch your step getting out.

Good advice, in general.

Down the steps and down the ramps Julius walked, somnambulistic. Through the huge dankness of the urine-smelling station, out into the twilight of Stillwell and Surf.

Det dødskolde Havskum, the death-cold foam.

Whither trudgeth our sweetheart?

To the playfield of his youth, the land of dreams where Freud had walked, a land once dazzling and now, in the after hours of civilization, only a rusting relic of its original. Humankind cannot bear too much unreality.

The road of life had led him back to his beginnings, and he felt a kind of giddiness vis-à-vis his own demise on the southwest tip of the long island, the long, old island, the sun sinking into the west, into the waters of Gravesend Bay. *Passus, et sepultus est.* Closing time.

Was it here on this rabbit spit of land that Freud perceived that "the goal of all life is death"? These ghostly force fields innocent of intellect, these subversive projects for the transformation of culture, these grand evasions of the Reality Principle, with their incessant music of structure and change and decay, as familiar as tears—could the good doctor not have sensed their muted trajectory toward the great repose?

Julius could recall the crowded beaches, now contaminated and empty. On his childhood summer Sundays, this sand and surf had been the most densely-peopled portion of the planet. Ten million bundles of appetite a year, ten million creatures of bingo halls and concentration camps, escaping from the contagion of history, from the blighted past, from the imbecilic botchery. Escape. Escape to irrationalia, escape from the blindness of vision and visions, the ideologic constructions visited upon the world, escape via antigravitation, mass ascension the direction, forty-five seconds up the Parachute Jump and ten seconds down, gravitationally weightless, perhaps morally weightless as well. The *moto spirituale* of Dante, was it not?—a forward dreaming into experience so bright that all details go pale? Then, riotous quiescence of appetite and self-destruction. The truth of the lie—would not the doctor have sniffed that out?

Ocean sounds, those good old friends. The in and out of eros and thanatos. Julius heard it now; would not Freud have heard it then?

• • •

Past the parking lot that once was Dreamland, past the weed-choked, garbaged field that once was Luna Park, that breeding ground for twelve hundred upward thrusts, towers, minarets, and domes, now grounded, gone to seed. Up, and down, in flames.

Julius thinks of his childhood blocks, of knocking his towers down in tantrum, or tweaking his Satans off them for the Fall. He remembered building his own Tower of Babel to wedge beneath the ceiling. Did that one fall? He thought not.

Whither wobbles our sweetheart?

Some Infrequently Asked Questions

(about the whither where our sweetheart wobbles)

1. What did Dr. Freud think of Coney Island?

Thirty-eight years before Julius was born, Dr. Freud came to Coney Island. He brought with him the thought-forms of Dreamland, of Drugs, of Death. He wandered through Coney's various capitals of ego, libido, and id and strolled along the Freud-unlimited midway. He hated it.

What might have been sublime was just unreal. Fake, fake, fake. Paint peeling off a hackneyed, clichéd world. Hell, he thought, was especially badly done. (He ought to know.) Fake brick, Old Nick, hooked wings, chipped nose. Inside, a red papier-mâché underworld, with ludicrous devils in red tights, angels with predictable harps and wings, imps—and none of perversity. Infantile tableaux of sin—American style: a young man eternally damned for drinking whisky, or for smoking a cigar, or—unlike himself—for playing ball on Sundays. A young woman primping before a mirror, fiendlets rising up behind her. The mirror becomes her casket. She screams ("Oh no! Oh, horror!") and disappears in smoke and fire. *Langweilig! Oberflächlich!* No subject has such dreams.

And all the disasters! Scene after scene for apocalypse-addicted people, scenes feeding souls upon the hideous. He was led through the fall of Pompeii, the San Francisco Earthquake, the burnings of Rome and Moscow, through three naval battles, and two episodes from the Boer War; he took in the Galveston Flood and the eruption of Vesuvius—"realized," the guidebook exclaimed, "with scenic and mechanical equipment coupled with a most extraordinary electric display—new inventions put into practical effect." Was this the way to exorcise nightmares—or to create them? Such nurture of the American mind, he thought; where would it lead? Lurking here was *something* intelligible, some essence wrested from obscurity, in some forgotten language. But such ignorance of fundamentals would never make for freedom!

One visit was enough.

Twenty-nine years after Sigmund Freud died, an anonymous hand, on the verge of another closing time, had scrawled on a wall in Paris: "America is the only nation in history to go from barbarism to decadence with no civilization in between."

2. Did Dr. Frankenstein also come to Coney Island?

It was not Dr. Frankenstein but his exemplary twin brother, Dr. Couney. Forty-four years before Julius was born, Dr. Martin Arthur Couney, en route from Berlin and Paris, brought his *Kinderbrutanstalt* to America—and stayed. A "child hatchery," with its stork on the gabled roof and its "nest of cherubs," was a magnet for a steady crowd of poor and childless women.

It wasn't money that drove him. He never took a cent from the parents (most of whom could not afford to pay), and the dimes offered up at the door, warm from palms and purses, barely met expenses.

For inside the "old German farmhouse" near the Surf Avenue entrance, Dr. Couney, inspired by the rearing of poultry, had built a facility more modern than that of any hospital in New York. Tiny infants, diapered pink or blue, sightless and feeble, lay in immaculate rooms, in gleaming, temperature-controlled, filtered-air wombs, finishing out, hatch-as-hatch-can, their incomplete gestations. Technology to the rescue—and milk from breast or nasal spoon or tube;

nurses wet and dry always in attendance; doctors always on call: the hatchery saved 6,500 of the 8,000 babies placed in its care, a record far unmatched by disapproving standard medicine, and a crucial spur to modern pediatrics. In that building, with its bogus exterior, surrounded by catchpenny monstrosities and the clanking of chains, there came to pass the resurrection and the life.

Four years before Julius was born, the incubators shut down. What had been revolutionary in 1903 was old hat forty years later, and attendance had dwindled beyond repair. America marched on. The New York Medical Society presented Dr. Couney with a platinum watch.

3. Did Dante come to Coney Island, too?

Mama mia! another immigrant, this one stoker of the Melting Pot, provider of the fire. Forty years before Julius was born, "The End of the World According to a Dream of Dante" opened at Dreamland. Creation in the east, Destruction in the west, only 150 feet apart, down Surf Avenue. His dream was big enough to need two stages in two different auditoriums, each holding 1,200 people.

The come-on was free and open to the public: at the entrance, a human forest and large reproductions of Doré's woodcuts, happily in the public domain. If intrigued, you paid your four bits and walked into the first theater.

There, in Victorian rocky terrain, a hundred men and women are speaking and singing a choral introduction, when suddenly the Archangel Gabriel appears, blowing the Trumpet of Doom, Mahler's *grosse Appell.* Darkness, thunder, lightning, chaos, a rain of fire upon a sinful world. Skeletons rise from graves and coffins, along with a few chorus members, wired up to heaven. Bad chorus members, the vast majority, poked by devils (red tights), are pushed, wailing and tumbling, down chutes into the fiery lake of Hell.

Incipit intermissio—while the cast scoots via tunnel, and the audience strolls via dim-to-radiant path to Theater Two.

In paradisum deducant angeli, sing the Fauré angels, *et cum Lazaro quondam paupere aeternam habeas requiem.* Jacob's ladder. Golden harps. *Exeunt omnes sursum.* Ascension. The resurrection and the life—ah.

For most, Theater One was more credible than Theater Two. Especially during and after the *real* event, for which the show was mere pasteboard rehearsal.

Kitschy as it was, and perhaps *because* it was, this Springtime for Satan left some with an itch for something more infernal. And for every itch there was a Coney Island scratch: Beyond the Dream of Dante, just past the Temple of Electricity, was Hell Gate. First you look, and now you do. Abandon hope, all ye who enter here. For two bits, those hellions who hadn't had enough of hell could embark in Charon's barge down a fifty-foot whirlpool to the gates of Hell, where they dropped into a twisting channel coursing through plaster-of-Paris displays of subterranean geomorphology—crust, mantle, and core. Not generally what they were after—still, interesting, and truly worrisome for family and friends left behind, imagining the worst. But the worst was worse than they could imagine.

In the wondrous month of May, thirty-six years before Julius was born, sparks from this gate to Hell set fire to Dreamland, and burned it to the ground. Tinsmiths had been using pitch to repair a leak in the whirlpool sluice—pitch, as in "he that toucheth pitch shall be defiled therewith." There was a short, the lights went out, hot pitch spilled over, and Loge came to play. Fire is a good servant but an evil master, and its hunger is immense. Four hundred firefighters could not control the blaze.

Dies irae, dies illa! First the stench of burning paint, and nasty fumes of insulation. Then the untoward smell of canvas aflame, and the nostalgic scent of burning wood. One could watch the upward growth, and then the reaching out, white becoming brown before bursting into farther-reaching flame. Hell Gate went, and then the Scenic Railway. Fanned by the gusting ocean breeze, great flaring sparks updrafted toward the tower. Six Couney babes were rescued from their building into the relative safety of the night. The Beacon Tower caught, story by story, 375 feet of pure white, with its 100,000 lights, the tallest structure on the Island, its eagle on the top tailspinning, no phoenix, but permanently to ash. Beacon Tower became a burning fuse, a windblown sparkler, a pillar of fire, frenzied, teeming, igniting buildings on both sides of the lagoon, visible all the way to the Bronx. And Satan was then toppled, Talmudic, consumed by his flames.

The heat became intense, the roar extreme. Lions and panthers were burning, but the roar of the blaze was greater than theirs—thunderous, harsh, prodigiously dark and deep. And the screams of firemen, and victims; and the spirit voices of the builders and consumers and of those who had birthed the country—Russian, Chinese, Portuguese, Spanish, German, French, Italian, Finnish, Swedish, Belgian, Czech, Slovak, Turkish, Serbo-Croatian, Bulgar, Irish, Dutch, Polish, Norwegian, Romanian, Hungarian . . . wail, "Ahhhh!"

Messes of mottage in cities of fire, ungraspable mix of vowels and consonants, vulgar and refined, fantastically intricate and abstract, never to be surpassed, ur-springing in primal leap to the infernal, brumming, becoming, swirling, mixing, fusing, blending, merging, and rising in convection's callous counterpoint and the obliteration of boundaries. Bushes burning, and the shattering of glass.

And then they were ONE, homophonic in a great, Götterdämmerunging pyre, a systematization of confusion and delirium, a rich choral harvest of unanticipation:

Ω
Hell
Gate Dr.
Couney's
Dumont's Airship
Under and over the
Sea Thompson Scenic
Railway Wormwood's Dog and Mon
key Show Shoot-the-Chutes Steel
Pier Funny Room Streets
of Cairo Mowgli The Missing Link Creation
Hiram Infant Incubator Attraction
The End of the
World Biblical Show Bostock's Circus Lions Pumas
Bears Wolves Leopards Hyena and Antelopes Ben Morris and
Haunted Swing His Wonderful Illusions Canals
of Venice Coasting Through Switzerland Japanese
Teahouse Maxium's Airships Temple of Mirth Leap Frog
Railroad Streets of Asia Trip
Over the Alps Temple of
Palmistry Rocky Mountain Holdup Show Hunting in the
Ozarks Shooting Gallery German Beer Hall
Freak Street The
Hereafter Battle of Submarines Deep
Sea Divers Altheer's Dog Monkey
and Pony Circus Conklin's New
Illusions Hunting in the Ozarks From New
York to California Trip thru Switzerland Pharaoh's Daughter
Village of Moqui Indians Pit Siege of Richmond The
Sacrifice Auto Tours to Paris Scenes of the World A Trip in an Airship San
Francisco Earthquake Show Circle Swing over the Great Divide Touring
the Yellowstone Feast of Belshazzar and the
Destruction of Babylon Bay of Naples The Tropics Arabian Nights
Fireman's Christmas Eve Bontock Head-Hunters Rigmarole The Butterfly
Mystery The Pandrome Alligator Joe's Cupid's Circle Novelty
Theater Glaciers Scenic Railroad The Diving Venuses Devil's Thumb
Village of Wild Men From Borneo Congress of Curious People Ocean
Wave over
Niagara Falls The Seven Temptations of Saint Anthony
Destruction of Lilliputia Pompeii . . .

. . . rising, rising, up, up, up, their flames pressing higher toward the sky in merry apocalypse, among blind, air-eating, nonsentient forces, dying in festivity, rising afterfall, firebirds unleashed, aloft on theorems of extermination. The whirl of the womb: atoms and molecules, fat and thin, dancing their reactions; mechanics, gravity, weight and weightless, density, heat flow, the moronic thermodynamics of inferno, the whole world turned into magnetic fields of gesture all pointing in the same direction—up—*judicare saeculum per ignem*—then down, in metamorphosis of something into nothing, resonant and deep, its ashes hovering like bats.

God does not speak good English. Perhaps He can't talk at all. Perhaps He can only act out. Not a good patient for Dr. Freud.

Dreamland became a parking lot, dance floor to pernicious clowns of speculation, a new chapter in demented survival of the useless.

Did Dante come to Coney Island? Decidedly so. And where in the waste is the wisdom?

4. And what about Edison? Did he come, too?

At last, a native American. Yes, yes, he came, eight years before Freud he came—accompanied by Westinghouse, and Faraday, and Adam Smith, and Death. They came to electrocute an elephant. Forty-four years before Julius was born, they came to electrocute an elephant named Topsy.

Elephants—the highest form of animal, symbols of strength and astuteness, emblems of wisdom, of eternity, of moderation and pity, removers of obstacles, charismatic beasts suggesting the power of Buddha: miraculous aspiration, analysis, intention, and effort. Their trunks are capable of both uprooting trees and picking the smallest of leaves, thus suggesting that humans develop their powers in both the gross and spiritual worlds.

Massive and gray, they resemble dark clouds of refreshing rain. Indra's mighty elephant digs with its tusks and reaches its trunk deep into the earth, sucking up water and spraying it into clouds which bring forth rain. Elephants thus link the heaven above with the chthonic below, and symbolize the mist that separates formed worlds from the unformed.

Their tusks, both digging tools and weapons, linking the beast again to things supra- and subterranean. Elephants were *named* for their tusks, from ελεφάζ the Greek for ivory. Achilles' sword, in Pope's Homer, had a handle "with steel and polished elephant adorned."

They are loyal and affectionate, the elephants. Older calves help younger siblings, adults their sick or wounded comrades. They demonstrate ideals. It is said that mothers of great masters will dream of them at birth.

Most easily trained of all the beasts, they rarely forget. And when their great patience is exhausted, they have a remarkable memory for wrongs done them, and many stories are told of elephant revenge.

Mice do not scare them.

Topsy was thirty, and weighed three tons. She began as a worker, hauling the beams and blocks that became the Island. When the parks were built, she turned entertainer, doing tricks, in pink tutu, for gawking faces. Toward the end, she became quite blind, having worn her eyes out looking at America—and seeing nothing.

But she did see the drunken trainer who put his cigarette out against her tongue and laughed. She picked him up, threw him against the wall, then smashed his head quite easily underfoot. Thus she became a "rogue," a "man-killer," and her sentence was death.

Topsy was given a bale of carrots laced with cyanide and scarfed them down without effect. Another helping, please? The park owners saw a chance to be tough on crime, and also make a profit. For every scratch, an itch: they announced that the murderous rogue elephant would be publicly hanged. "No, no!" cried the ASPCA. Too cruel and inhuman.

"No, no!" cried Thomas Alva Edison. Hadn't New York State just replaced the gallows with a new, humane, electric chair? "I'll come and help."

There was more to this than met the eye.

In Topsy-time the Wizard of Menlo Park was engaged in his own death-struggle with George Westinghouse for control of America's electrical infrastructure. His DC system, he claimed, was safe, while

Westinghouse's was deadly. To prove it, he'd been publicly electrocuting cats and dogs for years. It was he who had convinced the state to use Westinghouse's AC for its electric chair. So much and no more had he accomplished: an electrocuted criminal was widely referred to as "being Westinghoused."

So what an irresistible photo op was here! How better to demonstrate the danger of his rival's system than to roast a full-grown elephant? Dr. Edison brought a team of technicians and a film crew. On 4 July 1903, before a cheering, patriotic crowd of thousands, Topsy was led to a special platform. The cameras rolled, and the switch to Coney Island's powerful electrical plant was thrown. Topsy's short-lived hell-on-earth lasted only ten seconds. At six thousand volts. She convulsed, her hide began to smoke, and she collapsed. Applause. "It's a take." The great man showed the film to audiences across the nation to win his point, if not his contracts, and to help forge the created nonconscience of his race. Intrepid readers may watch this fifteen-second film in the privacy of their own hearts. Just google "Topsy electrocution."

Whither reeleth our sweetheart?
He sang to himself, in cadence count:

E non voglio più servir,
No, no, no, no, no,

E non voglio più servir, hitting on *vir* a low E flat—abysmal depth, and the base tone of creation.

Non serviam.

George Orwell had warned Julius some time ago: "We have now sunk to a depth at which the restatement of the obvious is the first duty of civilized men."

Whither hobbles he, wandering among these ghosts?

To the towering Parachute Jump, which—six years before he was born—had been transferred from the "Lifesavers' Exhibit" at the New York World's Fair, the site right next to the Centaurs. Julius liked the Parachute Jump. It reminded him of his father. "It packs more thrills than any wings-in-sky interlude since Icarus," the old guides used to say. It reminded him that it takes longer to rise than to fall. Its rising and falling came to an end in '68, on a nearly vacant lot, in a moribund park on Coney Island. And now, there, in front of him, it rusted.

For Hegel, the Enlightenment meant a struggle between reason and what he called "the night of the world," that chaotic mix of hatred and irrationality which can destroy humanity and what it builds, but which is paradoxically the source of its enormous energy.

For Hegel, human history revolves around the attempt to negate the negativity of "the night of the world" and turn it to productive thought and action. He would have liked to have said, “Where there is id there shall be ego.”

5. Final question: Which tense do you want to live in?

“I want to live in the imperative of the future passive participle,” our sweetheart said, “in the ‘what ought to be.’”

19.

The Death and Transfiguration of Julius Marantz

Climbing and climbing on the narrowing tower, the victim cannot hear the executioner. At least not yet. All Julius heard was the rubbery thud of sneaker on rung after rung, and the hoarseness of his breathing as the Surf Avenue traffic faded away. On 19 June 2003, fifty years after Julius Rosenberg and his wife entered death's dark place, Julius Marantz, wifeless, friendless, climbed the skeletal Parachute Jump, a relic of his past and of his good old days in the floating world. Encased in the cage enclosing the ladder, nitro under tongue, he was unafraid, and leaned back when breathless, to take in the view.

Ballpark down there, KeySpan, HOME OF THE BROOKLYN CYCLONES; there had been no such team, no such stadium, no such corporate naming in his youth. Then, oh, then, the field had been covered with the graceful towers of miraculous castles and temples, entertainments to stagger the imagination, strung with fairy lights blinking into the sea breeze, fabulous and beyond conceiving in these days of mere mendacity.

A biplane buzzed overhead, heading into the sunset, dragging a slogan behind it. "NIX 666," it proclaimed, and Julius's thoughts went from Nixon to Sonnet 66, *Tired with all these, for restful death I cry*—but he couldn't remember more than the first line. He paused halfway up to catch his breath, and ease his chest, and place another nitro under his tongue. For the first time, he thought of these, his final hours, as suicide, and not as fight and flight in a world of murderers. Suicide, yet without a plan beyond Anaximander's: "It would be best not to be."

But maybe he was just old now, and this was the just the voice of old: simply follow the lines of force. My life, he thought, is unworkable, inane. Everything I do contradicts its outcomes; every feeling I have entails its opposite. I'm core tired, *épuisé*. I owe God a death. It's time for annihilation.

As Camus once noted, there is a terrible cogency in the self-evident, and Julius shivered pleasantly at his first real whiff of nonbeing. Felt kind of good. Off with the scum on the surface of his soul!—*Ad astra per aspera.*

Climbing and climbing on the narrowing tower, the victor cannot fear the consequence. Three-quarters of the way up, harshly puffing, he stopped again to catch his breath. Man is an obligate aerobe, he thought, and pushed on ahead.

The sun sank into the sea as Julius pushed open the trap to the top, and pulled himself, slightly shaky, out onto the mushroom roof.

His breath was hard in coming. The quest for oxygen, he thought, the essence of freedom. Without oxygen, all freedoms withdraw, and I am afraid. He sat till bravery returned.

Pulling himself up along the banister, Julius, acrophilic, surveyed the twelve arms radiating out around him. Which? he thought. To the north, facing the great city? To the east, looking out along the old island that flowered once for Dutch sailors' eyes? To the south, over the dark expanse of waters? To the west, the land of evening and *Untergang?* He chose a southwest arm so he could commune with both city and sea. Inching out along the limb, he arrived in couching darkness at the pulley structure from which the chutes were lowered, undid the cable wrapping the faded green canvas, and lowered the chute and its seat below the steel canopy. Could he do it? Could he shinny down the cable, past the cloth, and into the bosun chair below it? Off to his right the ghostly, nocturnal holograph of the World Trade Center, now in the shape of immense praying hands, lit up the clouded sky. Philippe Petit sang in his ear, *"Allons-y, mon ami, allons-y."* Still . . .

But this was Creation as it lay, and who was he? According to the Upanishads, they that see variety and never unity shall suffer many deaths. Julius saw the unity in scheme, the compassed geometry, Galileo's pendular motion, and who was he?

Down he climbed, his act of virtue, hand under hand, Nikes prehensile beneath. Down below the radial reach of the canvas, down the cables, down into the sling of the seat. And there he sat, now belted in, swaying in his own momentum, the city lighting up to his right, the sea darkening to his left, the clouds clearing the sky. There he sat, waiting.

Waiting is a strange way to commit suicide, though common, perhaps, to all. Waiting in the remains of a parachute seat, in the graveyard of Coney Island, is not so common. Yet it captured perfectly Julius's combination of willingness and latent resistance, *la chute, et la parachute,* both waiting.

Swinging, singing in the gathering darkness, the singer does not make the melody. For what was he singing? Why, the old Kaddish from shul, a prayer for endings, an orison of praise, an embrace of human attachment. Ha! A death-seat conversion in the other direction. For his father, reflecting on the merits of Julius's apostasy, had once told him the joke about a dying Jew converting to Catholicism:

"Why?" his family implores, "Why now?"

"Better one of *them* should die than one of us."

The logic was Jewish and impeccable. Yet he would not make the backward leap. For nothing in this world was as poignant to Julius Marantz as Yahweh's desire to become a man in Jesus, God's search for wholeness and Self. The answer to Job: love is what we want, not freedom.

He gazed out into the free Atlantic, Milton singing in his head:

The secrets of the hoary deep, a dark
Illimitable Ocean without bound,
Without dimension, where length, breadth, and highth,
And time and place are lost . . .

Julius turned with teary eyes to the lights and show of lower Manhattan, "the nearest coast of darkness . . . bordering on light."

. . . where eldest Night
And Chaos, Ancestors of Nature, hold
Eternal Anarchy, amidst the noise
Of endless wars, and by confusion stand.

There, there sat someone directing his death. He had only to wait. Do you, Agent Marantz, take this woman to be? I do. I feel her growing up inside me, and I will be unborn. Einstein's ashes were scattered in the Delaware River. Though He may be functionally nonexistent, yet God is great, as is his mercy. Accepting death is not a sin, is *not* the same as suicide. I die, therefore I was. Voluntary death is my privilege as a man. Scattered.

His eyes became accustomed to the darkness. He peered out over the ocean with the eye of a nocturnal bird. Why is the sky blue, Daddy?

My father with his strong but wounded love, my mother in her narcissism. Perfect teachers for the mysteries of my days. And yet there *is* no mystery; is there? The mystery is only in myself, at the bottom-most pit of myself.

I only know that summer sang in me
A little while, that in me sings no more

It was only two days to summer solstice.

Check.

Julius felt a lopsided jerk

Check.

Lopsided no more.

Check!

The main cable snapped against the edge of the canopy. Julius realized he was no longer hanging down, but suspended out horizontally from the pendular axis of fall. Check, he thought, the final challenge to one's king. The penultimate word with its dry and chopped-off sound, like a guillotine blade striking the top of the frame. You may try to escape, but the end is likely near. Failure. Defeat. The story of all life.

CHECK

He looked behind and saw the main cable—snapped—swaying below the steel canopy as he himself once had. He watched his parachute float back beneath him, held by the ropes from his bosun chair. His head and shoulders led the way as they had at his birth, but this time upward, away from the earth. At his buttocks, belted to his waist, his chair, with its green canvas afterbirth trailing below, slowly filling with air. It was not unpleasant, this feeling of up.

Check.

The parachute snapped into full deploy, transformed to para*monter*, and Julius's ascent slowed, as if dropped into lower gear, a sweeter transport, smoothing out betrayals and leaving deathstink behind, below. Julius looked down to the sea and the ghostly sand. I have known only the back of the world, he thought, the brutal, bear-like back of things. And now I travel around to the front, perhaps, to their face. The mysterious thing about death is that it is not mysterious. The road to the open. But the open is not open. I am, I shall not be.

Dread arises. What expression is on my face? Saint Catherine said, "All the way to Heaven is Heaven."

But the silence was blaring, with the spreading stillness a too-mild stir of former flux. Julius felt his power slipping from him, slipping away with his name and numbers. As air density decreased, his upward velocity intensified, the paramonter exerting less drag, and less, and his speed becoming growth and juncture. The aleph hush before the thundering word, stillness on an immense plane, the resonating chamber of nothingness.

Goodnight stars,
goodnight air,
goodnight noises everywhere.

His face, his final face, now shutting down at the boundary between staying and passing, dissolving into the house of death. You always were a nothing, now be not. The ultimate check.

Grrreck.

The death rattle, spasming muscles in the voice box of the newly dead. Man is an obligate aerobe, and death agonies are merely muscle twitches induced by terminal blood acidity. Where was Julius? Find Julius. He might be that angel moving etherically on spreading wing. He might. He might be floating into freedom. There was, no doubt, the process of suffocation: his pulse quickened, his blood pressure jumped, and his pCO_2 rose rapidly to hypercarbia. Julius, it's OK. It's *hypercarbia* that makes you anxious. Also cyanotic. It's OK.

Julius made increasingly strenuous attempts to pull in more air, but there was only less and less to be found. Those below imagine a kindly supervening unconsciousness triggered by the unoxygenated brain. They watch the breath become weaker and more shallow. They note the irregular heartbeat, and finally its cessation. Too far away they are to feel the synaptic relaxation, the rich tectonic shift into a safety beyond variety or promise. What they don't understand is the disappearance of the great sucking hole, ever aching to be filled.

Pegasus was rising in the late-night sky. Pegasus of the moon-shaped hoof, Pegasus, moon horse, steed of the Muses, pack beast of lightning and thunder, Pegasus rising. The great horse Pegasus abandoned this world for a dream.

Julius's trajectory was directly into the great square, that window opening into nothingness, normal to the galactic plane.

"Cede Deo," he cried, and *"Shema Yisroel. Shema Yisroel, Adonai Eloheinu; Adonai Eckud! Baruch shem kavod malchuto leolam vaed! Ewig, ewig.* Too beautiful to be believed."

Inside to outside, outside to in, the economy of vastness in the vasty hall of death. Gray-eyed Lydia, his inner zodiac, the cross-dragging foot, and gashing the sky. Burn, O Mind Divine, and consume all imperfection.

Borders open on all sides, stillness within stillness resounding in second immensity. No further need of a vessel. He belched his crimson life out into the chaste sky, intangible, nocturnal, yet not of night Expansion-shaped, he entered into death's dark place, and sent his photons out into the world The power is rising in me, i shall be sunlight soon, i feel, wafting, jerusalem, surging,

Julius and His Friends

This book had its inception in the odd monument on the Middlebury College campus, referred to on page 26. Now what the hell was *that* all about? The blessings of gravity research?

I imagined a story quite similar to the one that turned out to be true—some rich anti-gravity nut offering money to the Physics Department, the department snagging the bucks, and then putting up a stone, thank you very much.

A friend of mine, Beverly Red, and I, sat down to try our hand at *Rapture Wrap,* a screenplay about such a tale, with me responsible for the Julius/science/politics stuff, and she for a counterpoint story of Olivia, his radical feminist filmmaker girlfriend, intensely jealous of Julius, going off to form a utopian Womensland in opposition to Julius's collapsing world. The screenplay, as do 99.5% of them, never made it past the xerox machine. Beverly and I each moved away from Middlebury, and Julius, like an abbreviated Rip van Winkel, went to sleep for a dozen years.

With the rise of the radical Christian right, its embrace by the powers that be, and the spectacular publishing phenomena of the *Left Behind* series, I thought it time for a satire on the Rapture, the religious dystopia which might result, and the manipulation behind it. I dissected "my" parts of Julius out of the screenplay, and spun them out into the novel you have in hand.

Once I discovered it was Roger W. Babson who contributed the money and put up the stone, the first thickening came by way of R.C. "Rip" Rybnikar, the archivist at Babson College, a business school in Wellesley, Mass. Rip (now one of my favorite, wildest bloggers) gave me many details, sent me lots of stuff, and most importantly, handed me off to David Kaiser, a double PhD in theoretical physics and the history of science. At a nice Thai lunch in Cambridge, David shared with me his sense of how the Babson craziness had actually changed the path of scientific research by teasing gravitational studies (with big-at-the-time bucks) out of the shadows of neglect and back into the mainstream of the discipline. (see David Kaiser, "Roger Babson and the Rediscovery of General Relativity," in Kaiser, *Making Theory: Producing Physics and Physicists in Postwar America*, PhD dissertation, Harvard University, 2000, chapter 10.)

Not being up to the real physics myself, I homed in on a quantitatively ridiculous, but qualitatively plausible mechanism for the Doodad, using the notion of nuclear magnetic resonance, a concept I'd absorbed from Tom Ferbel, a college physics buddy for whom NMR shined as a beckoning star. He has since become the top quark at the

D-Zero collider at Fermilab, and was recently appointed manager of the US Experimental High Energy Physics Program at the Large Hadron Collider at CERN. Thus, unlike me, he has a real job, and gets to travel to Geneva. In spite of the book, we are still friends, with himself providing me with non-binding propositions about reality.

Many other real world friends have found their way into Julius's life. Ed Braverman's dog, Yenta, did actually have a well-advertised bark-mitzvah in Boston in 1983. Ed himself is a novel waiting to happen.

Aage Nielsen was inspiring. As an experimental educator in the early seventies, I spent a Christmas with him at his New Experimental College high up in Denmark. Nisseman and gadfly extraordinaire he surely was, inspiring and daring, and I cribbed much of his language for young Julius to consider. He died in 2003, at the age of 83. The world of education—and the world at large—has yet to catch up to him.

Elka Schumann, besides being the matrix of the Bread & Puppet Theater, has single-handedly, it appears to me, brought the world of Sacred Harp singing back to its roots in New England. A little group, sitting around her kitchen table in Glover, Vermont, spawned Larry Gordon's Word of Mouth Chorus, whose tours and recordings have seeded the formation of hundreds of other Sacred Harp groups. All the choruses running around in Julius' post-Rapture world are singing parts of the many tunes we have sung at local "sings". I met my wife at one of them. Word of Mouth choristers will play themselves in the movie.

As with Charles Ives, Malcolm Goldstein was the violinist who taught me about Messiaen, as we worked up a performance of his amazing *Quartet for the End of Time.*

Fred Ramey, my editor at Unbridled, has once again put his masterly hand to an unruly text, and, insisting that I be a better writer than I am, helped turn Julius from a comic novel with serious undertones to its converse.

Finally, of course, my faithful Donna, who puts up with all this, critiques the work, and even puts food on the table.

Thank you all.